SPARTACUS

Adrian Franklin

SPARTACUS

73 v. Chr.

IMPRESSUM

Spartacus
Novel
von Adrian Franklin

Autor: Adrian Franklin
Kontaktdaten (Haupstr. 86, 51143 Köln)

Herstellung und Verlag: BoD – Books on Demand, Norderstedt
ISBN: 9-783746-03515-4

Buchcover und Illustration:
   „die gladiatoren-001", Peter Beissert (Atelier Beissert)

MIX
Papier aus verantwortungsvollen Quellen
Paper from responsible sources
FSC® C105338
FSC
www.fsc.org

About the Translation

The novel was originally written in german language. The translation was done by me, some friends, and people I met on my travels.
There is no preference between british and american English, it was decided by: How common, how well known, the chosen form appears, (for example: „centre" not „center" or „behaviour" not „behavior").

T. G. *a german-israeli author, writes in broken german language.*
Perhaps, without knowing it, I wouldn't have done it this way.

table of contents

Prolog

„...some are marked out for subjection...
he, who is by nature not his own but another's man,
is by nature a slave; and he may be said to be
another's man who, being a human being, is also a
possession."

Aristotle, Politics, 1254b16–21.

Year 73 B.C.

Nothing indicates to a insurrection when a small
group of gladiators manages to escape from the
school in Capua. Rapidly a conflagration develops
that spreads across the whole country.

Under the leadership of the Thracian Spartacus,
they defeated the roman armies, victorious all over
the world, time and time again. For almost three
years, they mastered the italian peninsula and the
centre of the then world power, Rome.

Chapter 1.

Thrace

The third hour after sunset. Warm fog, illuminated by the moon, lies on the valley, covering the battlefield.

By early evening both armies had met on a high, treeless plain, ten thousand Thracians against thirty thousand Romans. The battle lasted only a few hours. The Thracians fought with changing fronts, behind which they retreated again and again in order not to be surrounded. Eventually their resistance collapsed. A small number managed to escape, about a thousand were caught, the rest lies dead or dying in the valley.

Next to the valley, upon a hill, a group of horsemen, among them the Tribune Marcus Glabrus. He had been sent to the southern frontier of Macedonia, to invade Thrace, as he had done two years before, defeating the Thracian tribe of the Maider. The territory of the Maiders was incorporated into the roman province of Macedonia. But the Thracians rebelled, not wanting to resign themselves to the subjugation of their territory, whereupon Glabrus was again ordered to ensure ›order‹. For the time being he has succeeded, temporarily there will be no more unrest here.

He gives his horse a slight nudge with his heels, reluctantly the animal starts to move. The group rides towards one of the camps set up by the legionnaires near the battlefield. Glabrus is wounded and his commanders urge him to get care, but he won't, knowing what the legionnaires hunger for. Then he hears it, the screams of women and children.

It's always like that, after the battle. Where he is near, they keep back, so he keeps moving, letting the horse trot through the crowd. A few more hours, he hopes, and they'll have drunk enough, be tired, and head for the tents.

While there is a law that dictates the survivors should be treated with care, because they are being sold into slavery and Rome needs the money, but he knows that he can hardly afford to impose punishments. Allegiance, fighting morale of the army, would be poisoned and difficult to win back. Even among his Centurions there are many supporters of these assaults and the legionnaires understand it as part of the deal, for the willingness to risk life, to go out for robbery from the defeated. To rob, to use, to misuse, everything that makes life, existence, alive again, women included.

Someone calls out to him, a voice familiar to him: »Tribune.«

He looks around and recognizes the silhouette of a horseman coming towards him.

»Yes, it's me«, he replies loudly. When both are already very close, he recognizes one of his Centurions.

»Tribune.«

»Centurion.«

»At the camp, a little way down the road, they're starting to torture the prisoners. You'd better come along.«

Even as they ride up, they hear the noise. Waves of whooping howls run through the camp. Feasting on the feeling of victory, they follow the greed, to inculcate them, with whom they are dealing, punish them for having risen against Rome.

A sound, a scream, sticks out of the din, not immediately recognizable as human. But then, in shrill, high octaves, undoubtedly one of the prisoners. Glabrus looks fixedly into the centre of the circle, a few more steps, then he sees what he has already assumed. A swollen back, swollen like a bruised peach, the skin torn. The man faints. Water is poured over the blood-soaked body. The crowd shrieks and cheers the tormentors on to continue. They don't intend to end the spectacle either, just loosen the strands of the whips from each other, as they are somewhat stuck together, and the knotty straps fly back onto the victim.

But the din dies down, gradually. Marcus Glabrus has entered the circle, not everyone noticed immediately »Untie the man«, he says, his face frozen, »and have him bandaged. Put the others on the wagons, chain
them and double the guards. Centurion!«

The addressee proceeds to carry out the order.

»Whoever even tries to get close to the prisoners«, Glabrus to the crowd again, »will be chastised by me, personally!«

A deep murmur goes through the round. »There would have been no such thing under Sulla«, says one of the bystanders.

»Step forward soldier so I can see you!«

Slowly the man steps out of the crowd.

»Tell me your name!«, coldly glares Glabrus him in the eye.

»Severus Verulanus, son of Vettius Verulanus, of Capua.«

Glabrus hesitates. Capua, if contempt for slaves has a name, then Capua. No other city where slavery is as widespread as there. The training of gladiators has mutated into perfectionism, the school of Lentulus Batiatus known throughout the empire. The training of gladiators has mutated into perfectionism, the school of Lentulus Batiatus known throughout the empire.

»I don't care what Sulla would have done«, Glabrus retorts sharply. »He is not here, but I am. The prisoners are roman property and to be treated accordingly!«

Glabrus glances around, then back at Severus, »get out of my sight.«

He lets his eyes wander over the crowd, searching to see if anyone else is willing to flirt with him, but no one dares.
He leaves the circle, along with his Centurions. »Let them keep getting drunk. Another hour and then they'll probably be tired heading to the tents. If there's trouble, have some of them arrested.«

»Yes Tribune.«

Glabrus gets back on his horse and lets it trot slowly alongside the others. *Why did I let myself be persuaded again?*, he asks himself. These wars, as Rome now wage them, can wage them, are repugnant to him. And then Sulla, with him it had begun. Since the plundering of Athens, this ›compensation‹, as some cynically call it, has been part of it. No, it was not a plunder, but a slaughter. It was one of the first wars of Rome with a standing army, a year they besieged the city.

Offences against discipline were punished draconically and the rift between Sulla, the commander, and his legions was inevitable. But he needed them if he was to hold on to Rome - so he let go of the reins when the Athenians surrendered, and like cattle the legionnaires descended on the city, murdering, torturing and raping. He had narrowly escaped death at that time because he had tried to stop Sulla from doing so.

Glabrus takes his dagger and presses it to his forehead. *Why do I always get this fever when I'm wounded? Those damned*

Marius worshippers, as soon as I'm back in Rome, I'll take off the title. I've enough, may they choose one from his faithful.

At noon the next day he gives the order to leave. After about an hour, the army begins to move.

Day after day, the entourage drags itself through the landscape. The ground, often so soggy that they sink into the mud, up to their ankles. Again and again bridges have to be built, again and again the army breaks up into several parts and only comes together again in the evening when camp is set up.

Finally, after more than two months, they have reached the Po-Plain. Here, on the paved roads of Italy, they are making faster progress. In about three weeks, Glabrus hopes, they will be in Rome.

When they are only a few days' march from Rome, a group of men on two-wheeled chariots approaches them. Glabrus, at the head of the army, suspects who is coming to meet him there. Lentulus Batiatus, head of the gladiator school in Capua.

He resents the appearance of these creatures, but respects such as these are inevitable. Gladiator games are becoming increasingly popular and the Lanista's need for new, strong men can hardly be met. Prisoners of war are especially sought after, because they are familiar with handling weapons and the Lanista can have them participate in the games after only a short time.

»Hail Marcus Glabrus, your glory precedes you. I heard you were victorious.«

Glabrus returns the greeting with a slight nod. Batiatus knows his reputation and expects no reply. But for his project it seems necessary to him to produce the flattery appropriate to his status. »With your permission, I would like to pay my respects. Finest silk. Finest silk...«

»The captives are sold in Rome«, Glabrus answers dryly, looking ahead, at the horizon.

Can't be helped, thinks Batiatus, greets the Tribune once more and continues along the human chain. Somewhere in the middle, the prisoners will be found. Despite the expected rejection, he still wants to know what will be offered on the market tomorrow. What he sees makes him happy. *Not bad, better than I had hoped.*

A stir runs through the thousand or so people Batiatus has his eye on. They have been gawked at from all sides since their captivity, but never in this way. One of the men pulls on his chain to signal to the man in front of him that he wants to talk to him: »What is this one looking for?«, he asks with a dry throat.

»I do not know. Might be a Lanista.«

»What does that mean?«

»A man who runs a gladiator school, a place where they train you to fight, in an arena until you yourself...«

»Yes, I've heard of it.«

»Then why you're asking!?«, says the other in an angry, broken voice.

»Hoped you'd say something else.«

Chapter 2.
Gladiator-School

The merchant ships drag themselves sluggishly up the Tiber, loaded with raw materials and precious items from the occupied provinces. Bricks, fruit and wine from Italy, grain from Egypt, oils from Arabia, game, wood and wool from Gaul, dates from the oases, marble from Greece and Numidia, lead, silver and copper from the Iberian Peninsula. All imaginable stimulants flow from here to the markets, making life a daily balm if you belong to the knightly or senatorial rank.

Impatiently, Cato waits for the captain's signal as he stands at the stern of the ship. *If only he would finally dock, what is he waiting for.* He looks down the river, past all the other ships following them. Looking at his own again, it seems much smaller to him than when he left Alexandria. Finally, the ship docks. Cato helps his old teacher Gawain across the narrow gangplank. Gawain, a philosopher from Alexandria, is reluctant to let Cato help him, even though he knows that he would hardly get across the gangplank alone. But without Cato, he would order the ship to be moored to the hawser until even an old man could disembark effortlessly, even if it took days.

A four-wheeled touring carriage is waiting a little off the beaten track to take them to the vicinity of the Forum Romanum. From here they want to continue on foot, first crossing the Forum, then continuing to the house of Senator Sargon, Cato's uncle. Astonished, visibly delighted and raising his head again and again, Gawain allows himself to be led through the southern entrance to the forum at Cato's side.

They pass the Basilica Sempronia, in front of them rises the temple of Saturn.

Behind it, the view opens up over a large, stone-tiled square, lined on both sides by magnificent buildings. Standing between the pillars of the Temple of Saturn, they pause for a while to admire at leisure the beauty of this complex. But the moment is short-lived. Unexpectedly, they become witnesses of the probably most ominous spectacle that one can encounter in Rome. On a bier, carried by servants of the Temple of Vesta, lies the body of a woman, bound with straps so that no sound can be heard. The people step aside in silence. No event covers the city with such dejection as this. Cato urges his teacher to go on with him, but Gawain refuses.

»A vestal virgin?«

»Yes«, Cato replies coldly. »They will carry the bier to a small dungeon at the Porta Collina - and bury the woman alive.« Standing between the pillars, their gazes follow the stream of people as it slowly moves across the Forum. Finally, Gawain grabs Cato's arm and motions for him to move on.

After walking across bridges and shady alleys, they reach the house of Senator Sargon, Cato's uncle.

Flavius, a close relative of Sargon, and only a few years older than Cato, welcomes them joyfully. With his slightly bouncing gait, he comes to meet them.

Cato is not very pleased to meet him on this day and immediately inquires about his uncle.

»A vestal virgin was unchaste, she was condemned. Sargon had to be present during the trial.« Flavius's pronunciation stalls in Cato's ear.

A lightness, lightheartedness that does not want to connect with what happened at the Forum. »Let him! Let him! Don't care«, he hears Gawain's stern voice softly behind him as they are led by Flavius into the atrium prepared for their arrival.

Silently, they sit together for a moment. Flavius looks at Gawain, who has also been his teacher. The hair is long, a few grey strands have come in. The bushy eyebrows seem to be growing together. But his eyes are as clear and alert as ever.

»I see you haven't lost any of your whims!«, says Gawain gruffly.

Flavius winces, the tone of his former teacher still crushing him. He seeks Cato's gaze, but does not find it, noticing only that he himself is meant. He wants to answer, searches for words, but unable to counter the stirring of the sudden reproaches. Gawain continues, without even attempting to bridge his previous words: »The priests are the ones, they are seduced by! Everyone knows it!«

»You're talking about the vestal virgins?«, Flavius looks at him with a cautiously questioning expression.

Gawain doesn't answer. Grimacing, he bangs his cane on the back of his chair a few times. »Is there anything else that priests seduce!?«, forcing each word out overly clearly.

»They took a vow, a vow of chastity«, Flavius replies meekly, looking at him questioningly, his eyes fixed on his face, his jaw slowly lifting again.

»Stop giving me this insanity«, Gawain thunders on. »They are six, ten years old at the most when the pontiff chooses them, know nothing yet of what they have between their thighs. It is the pontiff himself and his priests who have their way with them. And then lead them down the dungeon to bury them alive.«

»She gets a supply of food, bread, water, milk and oil«, Flavius replies calmly but with conviction, his voice sounding like the recitation of a list of today's market offerings. He wants to continue speaking, but Gawain, of impulsive nature, angrily cuts him off: »What fool burned your brain? Bread, milk, oil, maybe they'll add a giraffe soon, it doesn't change anything. The dungeon will be filled with earth and she will perish there, suffocating, surrounded by darkness.«

Flavius stares at his former teacher, mouth half open. He wants to answer, but the old man's dismissive attitude destroys all attempts.

Leaning back, face averted and the corners of his mouth twisted fiercely, Gawain gazes into the distance. Flavius forms a few sounds with his lips, but doesn't get around to answering as Cato intervenes and gently takes him aside. »He's gotten older, sometimes short-tempered. You shouldn't take it too seriously when he talks like that. Besides, I think that such journeys are too tiring for him now.«

»Maybe, let's believe that's the case«, Flavius replies, taking a step toward the exit of the atrium.

»I'll go with you«, says Cato, »I'll take you as far as the gate.« Silently, they both leave the atrium and walk down the steps into the courtyard.

»He shouldn't be making these speeches outside the house«, Flavius breaks the silence, »It doesn't take much to condemn someone these days.«

»Understand. I'll tell him.« They both walk the last few steps to the archway. Slaves open one of the heavy wooden wings.

»Please forgive my awkward behaviour, I probably wasn't a good host to you. I thank you all the more for the welcome you have given us.«

Somewhat annoyed, Cato notes how expertly such phrases still roll off his lips, despite his years in Alexandria.

»It's good to see you again, Cato. You are always welcome.«

Cato walks back into the house. When he re-enters the atrium, Sargon, who has just returned, waves from the terrace. He seems to have become more corpulent, the senatorial purple stripes on his tunica no longer falling as low as they did a few years ago. The hair is ice-grey, but his eyes, as always, two narrow slits that never reveal too much.

»Cato. My Cato«, he greets his nephew in a bristly but kind voice, grabs his hands and squeezes them tightly, »nice to have you back with us.« They both embrace happily. »You've become a man.«

»I've been before.«

»Nonsense, half a child.«

»If you say so«, he tosses his head briefly aside shortly and pushes back a strand of hair. An obnoxious gesture, but it helps him suppress a slight grin.

»Where's your teacher? Gawain? Didn't you write that he wanted to accompany you?«

»The journey was very tiring, and then old age, he retire.« Sargon laughs briefly and contorts his face into a benevolent grimace in response to Cato's arguments about old age.

»Flavius welcomed us. It almost came to a quarrel, between him and Gawain.«

»So, why?«

»We were taken to the Forum and then continued on foot when the procession of the Vestal Virgins to Porta Collina crossed our path.

We were standing at the top between the pillars and suddenly they came, with the stretcher, - guess you know.«

»Yes. - Is there anything to worry about?«

»I don't know, he's become very strange to me.«

»Your teacher?«

»No, Flavius.«

Sargon makes himself comfortable on one of the benches and leans against the wall with a light sigh. »Not a drinking session he skips. Wasteful his expenses. An army of slaves cultivates his fields. The Cilicians cut off grain supplies more and more frequently, increasing his profits immeasurably. And like all patricians, he firmly believes that fate has chosen him.«

Cato suspects that Sargon's surliness does not stem solely from Flavius' way of life. »You're tired of court hearings, why do you keep attending them?«

»You don't understand, you're not old enough for that!« growls Sargon, grouchy as an old bear, but immediately grabs Cato's hand and pats it a little. He opens his mouth a few times, as if to say something else, but leaves it at 'ah' and shakes his head as if to excuse his own foolish mind. Mirsa, a slave of the house, brings a jug of olive oil.

»Have thanks«, says Sargon, »give the plants in the atrium some more water and bring me my toga.«

Both linger a moment, looking at each other. One would hardly suspect a philosopher in Cato's countenance, but under the black, tousled hair he is more likely. He is slender, but by no means skinny. *What drives this boy to philosophy*, Sargon thinks to himself. »Tell me finally about your journey and the sciences you have pursued.«

»It's not in me - to tell stories.« Cato's voice betrays his reluctance to speak of himself. »It would only bore you.«

But Sargon is not satisfied with that. He likes to step into this paternal role. »No excuses, my good nephew«, he tugs at his toga. »You wouldn't refuse an old man's request, wouldn't you?«

»I'll tell you about it, but first let me know what became of Tiberius. You wrote me they're going to take him to court.«

»Yes, they did. It was one of today's negotiations.«

»It was today?«

»The trial ended in an acquittal.«

»That's impossible!«, Cato rages.

»Impossible? No! He was charged with buyouts, election fraud, plundering provinces, and bribery. The machinations for which he was indicted brought him acquittal. Outside, his litter bearers were waiting to take him to the port. He will be on his way to Capri by now. And there, in one of his villas, his his female slaves will take care of him.«

»Possibly not only them.«

»So? You heard something?«

»In Alexandria. There were even rumours that captors went out after dark, looking for orphaned boys and girls.«

Sadness covers Sargon's face. »Let's go inside«, he says after a while, »the evenings are still cool.«

*

break the will

The sale of slaves is one of those events in Rome that does not require heralding to be announced. Especially when they come from distant lands, beyond the realm. They are offered, bound and naked, on a high podium for all to see. Cato stands apart, in the shadow of a house wall.

The sale drags on, there are always riots among the buyers, which leads to longer interruptions. Either they feel ignored and start shouting wildly gesticulating that they were not being heard. Or they feel betrayed when they suddenly see 'goods' on the podium that make a much better impression than the ones they just spent their money on.

A woman of unusual beauty is offered for sale. Still almost a child, Cato thinks and looks into the serious face. Her eyes look straight ahead, into nowhere. A tremor runs through her body and settles in her thighs. Her expression remains the same, only a swallow hints at how much she is struggling with herself. The trembling stops. Proudly she looks further into nowhere and Cato shivers at the idea of how this pride will be broken. He sees the faces of hungry men, saliva running from stinking, toothless mouths.

Suddenly there is great commotion. A group of slaves is desperately trying to follow the shouts of one man. On the right, the guards rush in. Defenceless, they are at the mercy of the guards' blows. Still the voice can be heard, the voice of a man who won't yield. Undoubtedly a leader among his people.

Finally they wrest him from the group, to tie him up with his arms crossed, to stretch the skin. Then he is chastised, his face turned to the crowd, the auction continues.

Tense, worn down by the heat, Batiatus waits impatiently for the men he set his sights on two days ago when Marcus Glabrus returned. As soon as it is their turn, he intends to signal one of his subordinates. Finally, after about two hours, Batiatus sees one of his chosen, a 'masterpiece'. The sinewy, muscular body shines in the sun, he still seems young, barely thirty. Like this! That's how he wants his gladiators to be. The Romans have long, since they cared who rips each other apart in the arena. They have to be beauties, warlike figures, as described in greek poetry. Amused, Batiatus notes that the women also cautiously turn their heads and crane their necks. Finally, he raises his arm and his confidant has understood.

In the evening, when Batiatus leaves for Capua, after having attended the auction for about eight hours, he can call one hundred new healthy men his own, for the sum of fifty thousand sesterces.

*

valuable

The gladiator school is located in the poorest and most run-down neighbourhood of the city. The large and solid wall surrounding the school, which also serves as the city wall on the east side, contrasts sharply with the crumbling mud huts that stand around it. Three gates provide access, one of them on the north side. Batiatus had it specially built so that he would not always have to drive through the dirty alleys, riddled with beggars. It is through this gate that he enters today, gives orders to feed the horses, and is led to his chambers, where a meal has been prepared for him already.

In the morning of the next day, as always, it is his task to examine the newcomers more closely. As he walks up the steps to the terrace, his steward, Leonidas, comes to meet him and reminds him of the visit of the two merchants from Lucania.

»They didn't have any questions?«, Batiatus wants to know.

»No«, Leonidas replies, »they have come for the ones we've sorted out.«

»Oh by all...,had completely forgotten«, Batiatus growls briefly and wants to continue, but then abruptly stops again. »And? Are the men ready for transport?«

»No, they are still in their quarters.«

Batiatus becomes frantic.

»Shall we cancel the reading aloud?«, asks Leonidas.

»The geographer's report? No! Tell Maecenas to lead the men out, everything as usual. Tell the two merchants they must be patient. Lead them to the east side, if they wish to watch the further proceedings, - they certainly will.«

Leonidas returns to the merchants. Exceedingly polite, he receives them again and leads them to the Tribune, on the east side of the arena. »The sun won't come over until the afternoon«, he says to them with a friendly gesture after they've inspected the facility. »Refreshments will be provided, of course, but also dates roasted in sugar.«

»Well, that's fine«, replies one of the merchants in a dismissive tone. »We won't stay long. We just want to look around a little, get acquainted with the customs of a gladiator school.«

Batiatus, meanwhile, has gone to the terrace above the arena, which is equal in size to the arena in Rome.

The newcomers are brought out. A group of wardens orders them to line up at a designated spot in the arena, then he speaks to them, with the wardens translating into their respective languages.

»You are destined, from now on, to live here, in the school of Capua, the most famous in the whole empire. You will be taught how to use weapons, trained to become gladiators. You should not be too sad about this. There are far worse things, as you are about to learn. And I pray to the gods never to have to send a single one of you to that terrible place of which this document tells.« Batiatus unrolls the papyrus and holds it up.

»It is a Greek geographer's account of the gold mines in the north-east.« He pauses to give the translators time, then he continues: »

›Beaten to work, whether sick, infirm, or a weak woman. Day and night without interruption. There is no way to escape, because everyone is tied at the feet. The guards are from barbarian tribes, so they speak different languages.‹

Do not think that this could help you just because you are also barbarians. It will be taken care that there will always be those around you who do not speak your language.«

Headshaking, now and then whispering to each other, the merchants watch the events from the stands. »What's all this nonsense about?«, one of them turns to the steward, his voice low, his tone irrelevant.

»The papyrus from which the words are taken was the report of a Greek geographer, Agatarchidas«, answers Leonidas. »On his travels he also looked around in the roman mines, the gold and silver mines. He died around here a few years ago, an accident, they say. Batiatus believes in fear. They should fear the mines more than death in the arena. We have a transcript here. Perhaps you like to see it?« The merchant, who had asked Leonidas, reaches for the papyrus and reads silently to himself:

> The quantity of people banished to the gold mines is very large, and all are bound at their feet and have to work day and night without a break. There is no rest for them and no possibility of escape.
>
> The guards are from barbarian tribes and speak other languages, so no one can be bribed by a friendly conversation or favours.
>
> The rock loosened by fire is crowbarred by tens of thousands of these unfortunates. By adjusting their posture to the position of the rock, they throw the chopped rocks onto the ground.
>
> They do this work continuously and under the merciless whip of the overseer. No one finds indulgence or rest, whether

he be sick, infirm, old, or a weak woman.
All are alike driven to work by beatings,
until finally, broken by the hardships,
they perish from their ailments.
Their misery is so extreme that they
fear future suffering even more than
the present, and the punishments are so
severe that death more desirable than life.

With a questioning look, the merchant offers the papyrus to his partner, but he refuses. While the guards monotonously translate Batiatus' last words, he climbs the stone steps to a landing, looks down the ranks and finally gives the signal to his men to start the first fights.

After half an hour he has to admit that apart from a handful of Gauls, Teuton's and a few Thracians, there is nothing 'useful' in there. In a bad mood, he lets the fights break off. The newcomers, who have proven themselves, are separated from the others, led through a labyrinth of corridors until they stand in a large hall. There they are forced to wash themselves. A doctor stands by to tend their wounds. Even harmless flesh wounds are carefully examined, anointed and bound. Everything is done to avoid possible gangrene. That's how valuable they are now.

The next day. Groups of forty to sixty gladiators are led into the arena. The newcomers are distributed evenly.

Each of these groups should correspond to a legion and like legions they should master tactical manoeuvres. Before the exercises begin, Batiatus climbs onto the stands at the southern end of the arena to watch the action from there. He checks the linen cloth stretched over him to see if it protects him from the sun, and lets his well-fed body flop down on the seat, raises his arm then towards his overseers.

With a stern expression, he watches every movement and pays meticulous attention to the correct wording of the commands. In a few days, emissaries from Rome are expected to arrive, to negotiate a price for his gladiators, for the festival in honour of Saturn is imminent. The highlight of the spectacle will be the gladiator fights and Batiatus hopes to be able to demand a higher sum in the coming negotiations.

The sun burns. Batiatus's enthusiasm has waned, half dozing off, he sits under his shady canopy. Suddenly, he winces because he hears a moaning, groaning sound. Excitedly he looks down into the arena where a circle has formed. Batiatus fears the worst. Quickly he descends the stairs and

approaches the men with quick steps. Maecenas , his guard, bangs his shield hard twice when he sees him coming, and the overseers form a lane up to the wounded man.

Batiatus' lips press together. The man's right knee is shattered. He is lying on the floor, shaking with pain. He exchanges a quick glance with his doctor: »He'll be limping, that's all I can do«, he says. Batiatus makes no reply to this, turns away and walks back through the alley.

»What was the matter?«, he asks Maecenas , whom he knows is behind him, »couldn't you cut off his hand?«

»You know we can't choose for long in such situations.«

»Enough for today. Let him be taken care of, maybe he can still be sold after all. A leg cripple can't run away that fast.«

*

Two riders from Rome arrive at his school this morning. Batiatus has been waiting for them for several days. It's one of the usual visits. It is mostly patricians who let gladiators fight at their extravagant feasts.

He has the men led in. They walk along the rows, examine the gladiators, ask questions, want to buy some of the new ones, though he refuses. *Always the same,* he thinks to himself. *They come a day or two beforehand to inspect the men.* This time he was on the verge of refusing them, reluctantly allowing them entry after all. There's no point in turning her down, it would only make everything else more difficult.

Coward

Time passes infinitely slowly for Cato, he longs for the day of his departure for Alexandria. At first he spent a lot of time with Gawain, taking him around town or having the wagon hitched, and they explored the area. They often spent the evening hours together with Sargon. They didn't talk much, they didn't need to be constantly chatting to be together. Now and then a question, a thought that was exchanged: ›A horse brings forth a horse again, never a sheep or a donkey. An eagle always an eagle, never something else, not even a species similar to the eagle. This is also true for us humans. But we sort ourselves after the birth, enslave other people, enslave our own kind,

although there is nothing approximately similar beside us. All thoughts

and reflections on the justification of slavery, may they be by Aristotle, I deeply despise them.‹

»But we humans are not all the same«, Flavius contradicted as he sat by one evening. »I'm not just a human being, I'm a patrician by my rank, I hold state offices, but I'm not a scholar like you are, nor am I a architect.«

»All fine with that«, Gawain had answered, »may the gods save us from a monotonous sameness. But the answer is already in your question. People should be distinguished by the arts they practice, the sciences, the professions they pursue. Here is truly found by what one individual differs from another. The claim to difference by status, by law, by birth, is contrary to this truth.« And it is precisely these thoughts, with which he undermines the existing conditions, that do not let him go. Three months now, since they sat like this and Gawain returned to Alexandria again.

His gaze wanders over the shelves of scrolls they've been referring to as he remembers Flavius's invitation to a tric- linium, given to him by a slave a few days earlier. Unde-cided whether to attend the revelry, he walks into the courtyard, wondering at the strangeness he suddenly feels, towards an invitation with an ordinary, usual occasion. Just two years ago, before he left for Alexandria, these orgies seemed like a welcome change. He doesn't want to be an ascetic, no! Though this kind of forced- out cheerfulness, squeezed joie de vivre, repels him more and more. He watches the passing clouds until someone gives him a light push. Startled, he turns around and looks into his horse's face. »Do you have to scare me like that?« He strokes his nostrils. »We might visit Flavius, just for an hour or two? What do you think? Then he won't be angry with us. It will save us a lot of explaining afterwards.«

*

available

Since the beginning of the festivities, Flavius has been trying to win the favour of the beautiful Valeria. After the guests have appeared in large numbers and he no longer has to lend his ear to the nomenclator, who keeps whispering the names of the guests in his ear, it seems that he has finally succeeded. The gladiator fights have begun, he sits down next to her, smiles at her, as if the choice of seat was only in the interests of the gladiators.

Valeria smiles back briefly, open rejection doesn't seem appropriate to her at the moment. But out of concern that her answering smile hasn't had the suitable look, she addresses him: »Flavius»«, she says, though without looking at him, »What a surprise, are you allowed to do that? Fighting to the death, here in your house?«

»Of course it's forbidden. Yet as you can see, these prohibitions don't apply to everyone«, he replies, trying to smile charmingly.

She smiles back. »I didn't know you were such a prankster.«

»Well - sometimes I surpass myself«, still thinking about the

›prankster‹ *What does it mean when she calls me a prankster?*
What does it mean? Why those things always so excruciatingly
indistinct over and over again? »I could show you around a bit
if you like?«

But Valeria ignores him, deliberately. No change in her facial
expression, her gestures, she stares ahead, at the group of
gladiators. *What does he want*, she thinks. *If I didn't look like*
I look... puts these beautifully grown warriors in front of me,
begging for attention for himself then. Her womb fills with heat.
But desire and longing also bring the rage again, an ocean of
rage, at mothers, at her mother. Ten years have passed,
maybe five remain. Ten years because she believed lies, from
women, from mothers, her mother, because she didn't know
about the anger of these women. They used her for their own
revenge. Had watched, revelled, cheered inwardly when men,
hand-some men, struggled to touch her once.

»Let me watch a little longer«, she says, even though Flavius
probably wasn't expecting an answer.

»Of course, my dearest«, and looks at her sideways, seeing
the greed in her eyes and feeling jealousy boiling up inside
him. He finally looks at the fighters himself and after a short
time he is sure to see the object of their desire. A young
Thracian, already fighting for the third time that evening, the
'wives' can't get enough of him, his body resembles the image
of Dionysus, carved out of stone.

Such a sight Flavius feels, again and again, as humiliation of
himself. Lanky, even sickly, his own limbs appear to him. He
looks over at the gladiators again, just as the Thracian is
stabbing his opponent when another's sword comes down on
him from the side.. With a lightning-like movement he dodges,

but loses his balance, falls to the ground, hurls his sword at the other, a twist with his body brings him back to his feet,

grabbing the sword of the one he had previously killed. *Like a cat*, Flavius thinks.

Cheering applause flooded the room. »Flavius, did you see that?«, Valeria tosses her head, wide-eyed and with an

expression that lets him know that her outburst of emotion is not aimed at him.

»He has the reflexes of a predator.«

He smiles and nods at her, but since she has no eyes for him, he looks ahead again and can clearly see the Thracian's face for the first time. He is breathing heavily, bitterness in his features.

He takes a step towards his opponent. Flavius sees the other trembling, the typical trembling of an overstrained body. Desperately, the latter raises his sword once more and delivers a powerless blow, which the Thracian deflects with his shield. Then, with a short, quick movement, he thrusts his sword into his heart. Thunderous applause.

The gladiators are finally led out by guards, and it is the turn of a group of musicians and dancers to entertain the company.

»Flavius«, Valeria turns back to him, thinking he is again seeking a conversation with her. Disturbed, he looks to the side, but immediately makes an effort at a friendly expression. »What do you wish, my dear?«

»I was just wondering, what does such a barbarian feel when he stands before us, as a victor, receiving our applause?«

»I don't know. I don't think he feels anything«, he replies with finality.

»Nothing at all?«, continues Valeria, putting a kind of naive unconcern in her voice to avoid any suspicion of concern for

this 'creature'. »Ooh, that can't be possible. One feels always something, anyhow, somehow.«

»I don't think they feel any more than a dog being slapped when he brings back the bone.«

»Haaa – hahaha«, Valeria laughs in her high voice, »my dear,

you never cease to surprise me. I never knew you could be so funny.«

Funny, she thinks I am, it burrows into his brain. He quickly tries for a smirk, but feels his face like a tough mask and fears Valeria might notice his discomfort when Leandros, his old house slave, releases him from the situation.

»Forgive my intterruption. Cato Livius Sargon has just arrived.«

»I will receive him myself«, and tells the slaves to set off.

»Excuse me, my dear«, he turns to Valeria, »I have to fulfill my duties as host«, he pauses for a moment, waiting for a reaction, but it remains with a brief gesture of her hand to signify that she has understood.

While Flavius makes his way through the left side wing, Leandros chooses a different direction. He has the same destination, but there are separate paths for slaves, beyond the terraces and verandas crowded with guests. Carefully, he descends the spiral staircase, passing through path-breaking round arches that lead past brightly lit baths and spas.

Purposefully he goes on, cursing the age that has sapped the strength from his arms and turned his fingers into useless stumps. He hears their voices again, voices of two adolescents from Flavius' annexe. *They're still busy with her, still*, he thinks.

»Do you like her?«, he hears the older one say.

»Yes«, he hears the younger ones reply.

»Come on, don't be so cowardly. You wanted it so bad!« Silence for a moment, then the older boy continues: »See the opening there, between her thighs? That's where you have to put it in. Wait, first take your finger and rub that spot, they like that. It makes them wet.«

Silence again for a moment.

»I don't know, - is it already wet – like...?«

»No. Reach for her breasts.«

Leandros listens, unnoticed. The older of the two is known to him. A raw, cold-hearted youth. Kept in the belief by family structures that he knows the opposite sex. Compelled to present himself in the guise of one who knows. The falseness that oozes out everywhere, fading the guise, must be buried. So he comes here to instruct a younger, to show him 'how to do it'.

Leandros remains praying. Praying to Isis, Zeus, the gods or whatever may be there, to give the girl the power to free herself in spirit until these unleashed creatures get their hoped-for result and let go of her.

*

'Ego' not absolute

Cato reaches Flavius' estate at a late hour not without intention. He expects the company already drunk, indulging in all sensual pleasures, wherefore they will ignore his appearance and won't come up with annoying questions, he can accept his invitation and leave more easily.

The rooms in the front area of the estate appear to be empty. He walks on until he enters a bright room, more of a hall than a room. His gaze wanders over the high walls and
  pillars that rise up into the vault. Suddenly he hears a sigh and a groan. He goes on, with slow steps.

Behind one of the pillars, he sees a woman lying backwards on the ground with a fixed gaze. Young she is, above her a bony creature of disgusting sight, which saliva runs from the
  mouth, while it greedily, sometimes sucking or licking, makes itself at the breasts of the woman.

Cato does not think, does not hesitate. Quick long strides, then a kick in the creature's ribs. Writhing in pain, it falls on its side. Flavius, who has made his way to receive him, can just intervene to prevent worse things from happening.

»By Zeus?! What are you doing!? Out your mind!?«

»The slave ring, I didn't see it! I thought the woman might be disgusted but too weak to fight back.«

»Disgusted? What does ›disgusted‹ mean here« says the one who was kicked. »She's a slave! A slave, nothing more!« He tries to half sit up, his face twisted in pain. »Where is she?«, he goes on with sick greed. »I want to take her. Or will you, who invited me today, deny me that?«

»No, no, my friend«, Flavius replies placatingly, »you shall have whatever you desire. Perhaps you want another girl? Just let me know?«

»No«, he gasps, with thousand-year-old greed, »I want only her.«

Cato grabs Flavius by his arm and draws him a few steps to the side. »What are you doing!?«, he presses through his lips, hissing, trying not to yell at him, as the sound amplifying hall might summon guests from the other rooms. »All this!? How can you....!?«

»It is, - as he says, Cato. She's a slave!«

Cato lets go of his arm. They both stare at each other.

»I think exactly like you in many ways«, Flavius continues, »a few hours ago, my cousin's uncle, Julius Catelina, was all over her. As disgusting a sight as what you have just seen.« He waits, for a reaction in Cato's countenance that doesn't come. »I can't have that kind of trouble«, he then goes on, »So I'm asking you, be my guest and act accordingly, - or...«

»Don't talk to me like one of your clients«, Cato retorts sharply.

Suddenly the room is filled with a wailing cry, undoubtedly a woman's voice. They run back.

As if in a frenzy of madness, the scorned man stabs the woman with a dagger. »You miserable bitch!«, he shouts, »you miserable hore!«

Cato wants to rush at him, but Flavius holds him back.

»Leave him«, he pleads, »for all the world, don't...«, but Cato tears himself away, grabs the raging man's neck, twists the dagger out of his hand and hurls the creep against the wall. Laboriously, gasping, he gets back on his feet. Cato moves next to him. »You better get out of here now«, he whispers to him.

»How dare you?«, he groans. »By the gods, I am a guest in this house«, moans and gasps. Flavius intervenes and speaks kindly to him: »Gajus, please let my servants accompany you, they will give you new clothes and cleanse you of blood.« Then he beckons to the slave girls who have been ordered to appear there. They take the woman's lifeless body and carry it outside.

»You fool, do you want to ruin me!? What's gotten into you«, he hisses at Cato in a silent voice, but he doesn't seem to hear him, staring spellbound in another direction: »What are they doing here?«, he asks dryly.

Flavius looks at the cage. The men inside have risen, standing side by side. Only the broad, massive iron bars separating them from their viewers.

»They are from Capua, the school of Batiatus. For once, I spared no expense. It was meant to be a very special evening.«

»Why didn't you have them taken away?«

»It would have been done long ago. But suddenly I got word you had arrived and - I had to stop you from kicking any more.« Flavius waits, but again, he cannot see the hoped-for effect of his words and continues to speak: »I never understood why you ascribe human sentiments to these creatures. They are barbarians, slaves. But you're right, they shouldn't be here. You came as the games had just ended and I went to receive you. It's a bit of an accident that they're still here and saw all this.«

»They have fought?«, Cato asks.

»Yes.«

Cato approaches them and looks from one to the other. »The second from the right, is that a Thracian?«

»Yes«, replies Flavius, »a coward, he whimpered like a woman. We had to whip him to make him fight.«

Cato looks at the Thracian and doubts Flavius' words. There is blood on his right arm, also on his legs, but it is not his. He takes a few steps forward and looks into the Thracian's face, who in turn is also looking at him now, his features stiffening.

»Since when have you been in the school of Batiatus?«, Cato asks him, waiting, to see if he will give an answer. »Does he understand what I am saying?«, he turns again to Flavius.

»Possibly, - I don't know.«

»Anyone here who understands Thracian?«

»You broke the old man's ribs! Because of a slave! – No, there is nobody who understands tracian.«

»It will be better if I go now, you mean?«

»You know«, Flavius replies, embarrassed, »you're welcome, but...«

»There will be trouble if I stay. Good, all right then. I didn't come to become a troublemaker.«

They both walk through the hall to the exit. Flavius stands silently beside him while a slave leads the horse up.

Cato suddenly believes he knows the face of this man. He looks intently at the angular features. On the left side, a scar runs from the temple to the middle of the head. Cato takes the reins from him and the slave takes a few steps back. Flavius dares him to take the wagon with the gladiators out of the house.

»You let him take care of the gladiators?«, asks Cato.

»You were just complaining about them still being in the house.«

»I feel like, - I know this man.«

»This is Rufus. I bought him from Petronius Sergius two months ago, he can be trusted.«

Cato has no doubts. He has seen this face before. Six months ago, during the auction, this man had been whipped, made docile. He had been recognized as a leader of his people as he tried to keep his people together despite the chains.

Today, with his posture bowed, his expression distorted into a friendly grinning grimace, he is only a shadow of what he was. The ›Ego‹ is not absolute, Cato recalls, as one of the teachers in Alexandria said, here's the proof.

He adjusts himself on horseback when Flavius speaks to him again: »As your friend, I tell you, your behaviour and your talk could become very dangerous for you one day.«

»Flavius«, Cato replies without looking at him, his voice full of contempt for all the contorted justifications of this class.

»You grew up in Rome, you know nothing else, - you poor fools. If you intend to flaunt such amusements again in the near future, make sure a cage like this is always well locked. Especially if that Thracian is among them again.« He pauses. Perhaps he shouldn't have said that, not with this allusion to origin, but pushes this thought aside then, even though he recognizes from Flavius' expression that he is waiting for an apology. May he be offended, it is all the same to him. He says goodbye with a short greeting and rides away. Flavius is left alone. He feels sudden anger rising in him. *Watch out for the Thracian. Isn't it enough that the women thirst for him, do we have to attach other attributes to him? - No, no Politeness and decency... is a way... always courteous and virtuous behaviour... appropriate to his status, what else could have made my mother... decide for my father... yes, of course , so it is...* Suddenly he notices Rufus, who is still standing next to him. With a short gesture he instructs him to take the wagon with the gladiators out and goes back inside, to his guests.

Rufus puts the wagon a bit off to the side, along a line of trees. The sky is overcast, it is very dark. He carefully walks around the wagon and finally stops in front of the iron railing.

He grabs the hands that are slowly reaching out to him. Silently he cries out into the night sky, again and again clasping the arms of the other.

*

Lentulus Batiatus walks briskly through the eastern wing of his house, nervously watching the play of light in the sun's rays. He wanted to leave early in the morning, now it's noon. In passing, he accepts shield and sword: »Everything ready? Are the wagons ready?«

»Yes«, Maecenas calls to him, already expecting him.

»Good, then we can finally set out. I'll be back in a week. Until then, no excessive drill, no punishment, no inspections of any rank.«

»It will be done as you requested.«

Batiatus looks once again at the entourage: Guards and about sixty of his gladiators, carried in heavy bronze-shod wagons. Then he gives the order to depart.

At dusk on the fourth day they reach the vicinity of Rome. He gives his entourage a longer break, also to have the gladiators cleaned and massaged again. As they try to pass the city walls, the guards block their way.

»What's the meaning of this?«, asks Batiatus sharply, directing his gaze at a short corpulent man of set age, whom he recognizes as a captain.

»It means that you must camp outside the city.«

»But I must go to the arena, I am expected there!«

»Not today«, the captain replies, and a broad grin settles on his fleshy face.

Red with anger, Batiatus turns away and orders his entourage to move along the city walls to find a suitable camp for the night. The next morning he is granted access.

Before the wagons with the gladiators are opened, they have to put their hands through the bars, each shackle is checked once again. Finally, they are led into the underground vaults of the arena. Batiatus is greeted by the Aedile in the usual manner, he is asked to take a seat and offered wine. In the light of torches the gladiators are examined.

Batiatus looks around. Besides him, another merchant is present with slaves of the 'delicate selection'. Humans, locked individually in bulky cages to force a crippled growth, for the satisfaction of freakish sexual inclinations. The price for such an 'outlandish being' can far exceed that of a gladiator.

Shuddering, he turns away and examines the arsenal of weapons, more out of embarrassment than curiosity. As usual, all types are represented. Shields, swords and helmets for Samnites and Thracians make up the largest portion, followed by nets and tridents for Numidians.

Batiatus reaches for the cup, glancing briefly at the Aedile. He looks at him disparagingly, with half-closed eyes, his long face tilted back.

»Why was I denied entry to the city yesterday?«, he asks him.

»There was a murder of a well-known city prefect«, the Aedile answers, putting pauses between the words, as if he wanted to start a new sentence after each one, to finally pronouncing the word ›city-pre-fect‹.

Batiatus understands the meaning of the answer only too well. ›Look, I'm a Roman, I'm an Aedile, I don't have to speak to you, I only do it out of pity. I'll buy your slaves, but we have nothing in common.‹

He struggles with himself, doesn't want to show anything, but it's harder than usual. Never before has he had to camp outside the city because he was refused entry.

Remaining polite, he goes on to ask: »What does the murder of a prefect have to do with my business?«

»The prefect was stabbed in his sleep by one of his slaves. Therefore, all slaves owned by him must be condemned. There are about four hundred, a large proportion women and children.«

»Did they try to prevent me from possibly buying them?«

»There is nothing to buy, they were crucified. There was concern about the many slaves in the city. Your creatures there pose an unnecessary risk, so I arranged to deny you entry to the city, 'till the execution was complete. But it went more swiftly than I thought.«

Batiatus reaches for the cup once more and briefly examines the Aedile, who has barely moved during the conversation. A sneer settles over his wooden face, his head still slightly laid back, one hand braiding around his pointed chin, he leaves no doubt about the farce of having him camped outside the city upon arrival. He has a preference for boys and girls, it is said.

Batiatus wants to end the subject and get down to business.

»Most of the men are very young - thirty thousand sesterces.« The Aedile gestures to one of the men in the background. »Here're twenty-five thousand, that's all I'll pay - and now leave us.« Another sneer on the wooden face.

Without hesitation, Batiatus takes the leather pouch and sets off on his way back. He imagined it differently. But instinctively he refrains from arguing with the Aedile. Four hundred slaves were crucified. At such events, the nobility reacts extremely irritated and sensitive to any form of slavery.

When he gets back to his people, he informs them that he will remain in Rome for another day or two, that they should set off without him, and: »During my absence, you will be under the authority of Apuleius.«

Apulejus, a tall man of sixty, was once wealthy himself. As a slave trader in Delos, he sold hundreds of slaves a day. To whom or where, was indifferent to him. Noble princes from the Parthian Empire came to his banquets at night, even kings dined at his table. For two years he has been in the service of Lentulus Batiatus. He performs his duties satisfactorily, but despises them deeply. Always tormenting himself with the question of whether it was drunkenness or superstition that drove him to ruin and made him a Lanista's servant. Sleepless his nights. He, who knew no scruples, now haunted by images of desperate families as the stillness and darkness of the night spreads, with its endless hours, during which he often reaches for his dagger to pierce his veins.

»Apulejus«, he hears someone calling. And then louder again: »Apulejus.«

He raises his head. Staring from deep eye sockets, he examines the man. »We can leave«, the latter lets him know.

Hesitantly, almost sighing, he answers, »Good.« Then, fully back from lethargy, he gives the signal to leave.

The roman guards open the gate. As the procession passes, Apulejus stays with the guards, hands over the pass and then hurries after his men. He lets the horse go at a light trot, since the guards are already closing the gate, he barely gets through, but yanks the animal back by the reins then.

Full of horror, with wide eyes he stares at the presented sight. Moaning and groaning, writhing in agony, the bodies of women and children hang tied to wooden crosses. Endlessly, the road before him seems to be a path of suffering. »They are only slaves«, it comes pleadingly from his mouth, »only slaves.«

But the voice of conscience is not content with that. Whipping his horse, he dashes forward along the train. »Cover 'em up!«, he calls out in a trembling voice as he passes the gladiator wagons. »By all the gods, cover them up!« Haltingly the train stops. Hastily, the wagons are covered with linen cloth, then driven forward again. Wildly waving his riding stick, surrounded on both sides by those dying on the cross, Apulejus drives the convoy, *if only this road would soon be over.*

Chapter 3.

Old Veteran

Before sunrise, Aedil Gratus rises from his bed. He was already looking forward to that day. This day, which is the last one, before the start of the gladiatorial games in the arena and on which a big banquet will take place. Fancy dishes are served to the gladiators, wine flows freely, women go from hand to hand. Whoever so desires can partake in these orgies of despair until dawn.

Gratus has the gladiators harnessed and crammed into the carriages. In the narrow streets, progress is slow. When the last carriage turns onto the Porta Lavernalis, he stays back a bit and waits anxiously. *Want to see how many there will be today*. Already the first wagon breaks out.

»Haaalt!«, he hears the driver shouting and steers his horse to the other side for he enjoys this sight again and again. *What a neck can endure*. »Look«, he says addressing the driver, »they're given a chance to fight and die like men, and then they cowardly stick their heads in the spokes and pathetically transporting themselves to the afterlife.« Watching the man's horrified face, he waits to see what he will do, to rid himself of the ballast that has been created.

»No! No! Not with the sword!«, he snaps at him. »You see!? The head is still on. So! Lift the carriage, turn the wheel back and pull that coward out.« Then he watches after the column which has meanwhile moved on. He should follow, but still remains in his place.

The carriage is laboriously lifted and the wheel turned back. He watches the dangling head with amusement. *Strange*, he thinks, *how such a head suddenly dangles from the body, not unlike a heavy ball on a chain that is a bit too short*. Finally he turns away and drives his horse after the column.

The head of the column has reached the south end of the arena. It swarms with people, surrounded by flute playing and the singing of pleasure boys, they indulge in the waves of orgy. Gratus gives his horse to a slave and greedily jumps on it. At late hour his body slaves try to take their drunken master with them, yet get kicked nasty by his feet. Laboriously they can make him understand that it is his will, since soon guards will be sent out to drive the people apart, to have the gladiators well rested, able for combating and waring, be combative and warlike.

*

whipping, burning

Senator Tiberius gives his sedan chair bearers a quick wave, he wants to reach the arena during the break. Rigorously, the bearers make their way through the throng. He closes the white curtains. *This filthy rabble, I can't stand these gawkers.*

Now and then he peers through a slit into the alleys, which are littered with merchants whose wares pile up under the projecting arcades of the houses. Passing flute players, jugglers, whores hawking their dances, the sedan chair pushes its way through the shimmering heat.

Arriving at last in the arena, he hurries down the steps to the ranks of the senators. In front of him and behind him incessant din. »Burn him! ... Whip him!.. Why does he go so fearfully toward the sword? ...Why does he not die joyfully?«

Too late again, he finds it uncomfortable, even hates it.

He feels glances in the neck, unbridled rage rises in him. Fleeing from all the tugging sensations, he throws himself into the rage of the others, craving for heated combat, for bloodthirsty battle. All afternoon he remains in the arena, clenching his fists, screaming his throat hoarse, feasting on the carnage that takes place in all imaginable forms.

Towards evening he leaves the arena. Visibly weakened by the exertion, he visits one of the thermal baths and, after an extensive hot steam bath, has his limbs massaged with warm oils. Finally, these hours are over too. Chased by his bustling spirit, he leaves the thermal baths, hole up into his sedan chair and harshly tells the slaves to set off, yet after short time, the sedan chair is stopped by guards.

»A fire has broken out«, the captain lets him know. »We've strict orders not to let anyone through.«

Tiberius pulls the curtains of the sedan chair aside, and the captain frightens. He recognized his counterpart immediately. In the light of torches, this face looks even more menacing. The oversized eyes, the pinched mouth, a narrow, protruding nose, all this on a head that is always slightly tilted back, reinforcing the fearsome impression. In a low, almost breathy voice, he answers the captain: »I'm Senator Tiberius.

So go ahead. Clear the way.«

»"I ask Forgiveness«, the captain swallows his saliva, but ultimately relieved not to have stuttered, not to have stammered, and thus not to have given a too obvious sign, which the character of this creature would easily interpret as

an affront to himself. »the fire is spreading very quickly. There is little water
in this district. It is mostly the houses of the lower classes. The streets are very narrow, so if a panic breaks out ...«

»I don't plan to spend the night there, now clear the way«, Tiberius hisses between his teeth. Then, without waiting for an answer, he beckons his bearers to move on. Quickly he forces them down the street and lets them turn into one of the narrow alleys. Young, dancing flesh he had seen here. After all the weary plagues of the day, he feels an insatiable desire. But the streets are deserted. Tiberius lets move on to the next bend and suddenly noise is heard, quickly approaching.

The street, here steeply sloping, gives view of the district below. Horrified, Tiberius lets stop. The city, to his right, a conflagra-tion, flames blazing high from the houses.

He looks around nervously. Whereas the narrow alleys were deserted a moment ago, they are now overflowing with fleeing people who are calling out in panic for relatives. Then, a house next to him, bursts into flames. Dense crowds now surroun-ding him. He orders his bearers to make a way for themselves.

Panic seizes him, which expresses itself in childish irascibility. »Out of the way, you wretched creatures!«, he shouts into the crowd, occasionally striking out with a rod at those who come too close to his sedan chair. Yet all his rage and angry gestures cannot save the sedan chair from becoming a plaything of the surging crowd. For a moment he thinks of handing out rods to his bearers, but immediately rejects the idea. This seems too dangerous even for him.

Suddenly he recognizes his bodyguard in the crowd. Catulus, his steward, was worried and had sent them after him. The five horsemen surround the sedan chair. Hesitantly, but more swiftly than before, the column pushes through the streets. Tiberius is relieved. Entrusting himself completely to his guards, he hides behind the curtains again, yet cannot stop the noise of the fearful people.

Then, suddenly, a long standstill again. Tiberius listens, but can only catch a few scraps of words: »Gladiators...need horses...wagons...smoke...up the streets.«

Peering outside, Tiberius recognizes the Lanista from Capua.

»No, no! Go on, go on, I say!«, he roars in a screeching voice. Batiatus jumps to avoid being trampled by the horses. He looks resignedly after the sedan chair. Eventually, he works his way back to his men with his strong elbows and tells them that they must try with only one horse. Since no one contradicts him, he hurries them up the street to the last of his bronze gladiator wagons. When he sees the thick plumes of smoke that are drifting up from a side street, completely enveloped the wagon already, he considers turning around for a moment, but heavy coughing can be heard. As the horse remains surprisingly calm, Batiatus lets them go on. *As long as they're still coughing, it's not too late*, he hopes.

*

Vault

Batiatus lost eighty men in the recent fighting in Rome, ten of them as a result of smoke poisoning from the fire. Ten gladiators who had proven themselves in the arena, a bitter loss that will be difficult to compensate. But replacements must be found for the others, as a beast-baiting is imminent. So he sends Apulejus to the optimate Cornelius Serbius, a

pupil of the patrician family and notorious for the miserable treatment of slaves, also known as a gambler, but of low intelligence. While his slaves toil in the fields, for up to sixteen

hours, always driven by the lashes of the guards, he gets through enormous sums in drinking bouts, accompanied by games of dice, almost ruining himself with the payment of bribes, in the elections a year ago.

Generally, Batiatus does this task himself. When it comes to select useful men, he trusts no one. But in this particular case, it seems to him that Apulejus should be sent. With his lethargic, slightly humble manner, he has the appropriate demeanour towards an individual of the nobility, ruled by a craving for prestige.

*

»So. You came to buy some slaves from me«, Cornelius' voice sounds angry, reproachful, mad. »What sum are you thinking of?«

»I would have to see them for that«, Apulejus replies in a cautious, subdued voice, careful not to question the patrician.

»Oh, her condition is splendid«, Cornelius goes on in his rasping voice, »you could hardly find better for your school than with me. The hard field work strengthens their bodies as well as your gymnastic exercises.« Suddenly he spits the morsel of meat he just put in his mouth onto the floor and calls out to one of the slave girls standing motionless in the back of

the room. »Get me the cook, now!« The moment he has
entered the room, Cornelius strikes him across the face with
a rod. The slave recoils, his right cheek seems to be torn
open, he throws himself on the ground begging for mercy.

»The flesh is as tough as the straps of my sandals again«,
Cornelius roars, red with anger, in hasty, overlapping
pronunciation. Then on, almost whispering: »But you're still
learning. By the gods, you're going to learn it.« Leaning
slightly over him, he stares down at him. »Out! Get the fuck
out of here!«, and turns back to Apulejus. »Did you see?« his
voice trembling with anger, »pathetic creatures, not an ounce
of honour.«

Apulejus is silent at first embarrassed. He knows only too
well about the distrust of this man, who feels quickly offended
by everything and nothing.

»Unfortunately he's only a cook, otherwise I would buy him«,
he answers cautiously.

»Don't worry, I've got what you're looking for«, and has the
horses bridled. Together they ride out into the lands. Still from
afar, wielding a whip, he yells at the guards, to gather the
men.

Apulejus examines them. Pale, emaciated faces are evidence
of poor nutrition, dressed in holey tunics, even in this rainy,
stormy weather. All in all, they are in a pitiful state. He walks
down the ranks, ultimately choosing twenty men. Without the
certainty of getting a particularly favourable price, due to
Cornelius' financial worries, he would have refused those as
well.

Back in Capua, Maecenas receives him at the gate of the
school. »It took you a long time. Batiatus was worried, he's

expecting you.«

*

»How many men have you got from him?«, asks Batiatus.

»Twenty.«

»Only twenty? That's not enough!«

»I know, I know, but the slaves of Cornelius are of little use to us. Even these twenty are rather ten too many.«

»We need more men for the games in two months. They need not be of special stature; it's enough if they can hold a sword. Didn't I tell you that!? They're just going to get eaten at these games anyway, by all these critters that the Aedile has gathered together again.«

»Forgive me, I ...«

»All right, all right!«, interrupts Batiatus brusquely his attempt at apology. »Go now!«

The weeks go by faster than Batiatus would like. Despite his best efforts, he cannot find the number of male slaves he needs. He sends for Maecenas to reassure him of the current inventory.

»How many do we have?«, he asks him.

»There are exactly one hundred and sixty«, Maecenas replies,

»we will have to add some from the main stock.«

»I had hoped to avoid that. See that, if possible, you take only some of those I bought at the beginning of the year when Marcus Glabrus returned. - And be careful not to hand them out indiscriminately. Maybe a hundred will be enough this time and we won't have to feed the others.«

*

Protected by a massive lattice, Batiatus watches the animal-baiting. The death screams of the slaves are drowned out by the howling of the masses. Already the first thirty are torn, hardly anyone found means to resist the animals. The ground of the arena shifts, and from the depths more trembling
slave-men are lifted. Driven by mortal fear, they run apart in all directions. But there is no escape, no elude from the beasts enraged by the roar of the masses.

Batiatus peers nervously through the grate, hoping the beasts will soon be tired and full, but the spectacle still continues. Pools of blood form in which the animals lose their footing. Some of their victims manage to escape once more and the screaming crowd feasts on the death throes of the desperate.

Again the ground moves and Batiatus' fears come true. Although three more lanista had been ordered besides him, who in turn supply the arena with slaves, it is not enough. Again the ground moves and Batiatus' fears come true. Although three more lanista had been ordered besides him, who in turn supply the arena with slaves, it is not enough.

He will have to sacrifice some of his already well-trained gladiators. Feverishly he looks into the arena, the beasts finally seem to be calming down, only a few of them are still chasing their victims, but most are tampering with the torn body parts. The noise in the stands dies down. Here and there the audience is already leaving the arena, eating animals are too trivial.

Batiatus descends the stone steps into the subterranean vaults. The gloomy corridors, illuminated by sparse torchlight, are engulfing the intruder and intensify the menace of the place, through the echo of the wailing sounds.

Slaves incessantly haul out the wounded, crossing guards leading other slaves to the slaughterhouse. A foul stench of scorched flesh, cold blood, and excrement wafts through the Labyrinth.

Batiatus holds a cloth in front of his face and quickly weaves his way through the crowd. He follows the guards, turns left into the eastern part of the vault and meets a Centurion there. After he has briefly informed him about the condition of his people, he asks about the physicians.

»Physicians? Take my sword, you'll be better than any doctor with it«, the Centurion replies with a mocking shadow in his voice. »It was sharpened today. Just one swipe. Arm or leg, it doesn't matter, just a swipe.«

Batiatus looks him over briefly and turns away without answering him. It would be pointless to argue with this creature. He dives back into the throng. The way back is difficult. Again and again the flow of people comes to a standstill, nausea rises in him. Finally, on the last step Apulejus awaits him and helps him up. »We will have high losses, the physicians are missing«, he lets him know.

»It's the second time this year they've dropped that part of the deal«, Apulejus replies grimly.

»It's that Aedile they put in place a few months ago«, Batiatus says, half to himself. »We can't do anything for now. Tell our men to get here by evening, that's how long it'll be before we get the survivors back.«

The next day, as he sets off for Capua, baggage train include, a delegation from the Aedile meets him on the Via Appia and asks him to accept an old veteran from Sulla's army into his guard. Batiatus suspects that this is more than a request and agrees.

*

»The men I bought from Glabrus«, Batiatus rubs his forehead, »how many did we lose in the arena?«

»Sixty-four«, Maecenas replies.

Too many, too many, Batiatus thinks, and continues in short, curt words: »Double the guards for the next few weeks, but relax the penalties for riots. The usual, you know. No gladiator fights for the next few months. In time, they'll forget about the animal baiting.«

»It will be done as requestet. But let me tell you something else«, Maecenas pleads, eager to present his success.

»What is it?«

»We singled out one of the men yesterday, - under torture he...«

»Under torture!? What's that mean!?«, Batiatus interrupts irritably.

»Forgiveness, it seemed necessary. The day before Saturnalia, when Apuleius brought back the men, they passed the crucifixion of the four hundred slaves.«

»By Zeus! Weren't the wagons covered!?«

»Not right away, they've seen everything. Since the survivors of the beast-baiting returned, we sometimes heard them talking about it.«

»Keep them apart. By all the gods, haven't I said it often enough!?«

»Sure, sure. But if we take them to meals or they do their exercises, we can't stop it. - Under torture, he confessed that there is a conspiracy or a secret covenant. That's all we could learn. Torturing another one of them would be conspicuous. I think so far they don't know that we suspect anything.«

»If it's true, then they know it too!«, Batiatus snaps at him. He turns away to organize his thoughts. *I shouldn't have stayed*, he thinks, *shouldn't have let Apulejus go alone.*

Maecenas - tortured again. Maybe right this time... ultimately too often... just on a whim. For Batiatus, with the rank of Lanista, gladiator school is more than just a source of income, but a form of expression, ultimately the only one. Physical condition of gladiators, their fighting morale, their fighting skills are ultimate evidences of his experience, his knowledge of human nature. Deficiencies, accidents, or failures, all disruptions of the daily routine were to be avoided at all costs. Those who buy gladiators from his school should not be bored by creatures lethargically rubbing their swords together. Maecenas is gradually becoming the antagonist of his finely devised system. *Maybe it's time to replace him*. At the time he seemed the right one. He was looking for someone whose appearance alone was deterrent. With an »allright then«, he turns back to him:

»Keep them away from the edged weapons for the next few weeks. Separate them regularly and place them in different quarters, every three or four days. And pay attention to the bookkeeping. I want to be sure next week who's been with us for two months or for two years.« He rises to retire to his chambers. »What else!?«, he asks as Maecenas begins to speak again.

»That veteran they foisted on you, Nicodemus?«

»Yes?«

»How long will he stay?«

»I wish he weren't here at all«, Batiatus says angrily, looking questioningly at Maecenas. »We could let him walk through the corridors at night«, says the latter, looking at Batiatus, waiting for a reaction in his face that prompts him to continue, »soon there will be negligence that we have to lament.«

»Good«, replies Batiatus, with a dismissive gesture, »I'll leave this matter to you.«

*

Slowly Nicodemus walks through the corridors, all quiet. He has been back in regular pay for a month, at the gladiatorial school of Lentulus Batiatus in Capua. Ten years ago, he was one of the veterans in Sulla's army. Today, at almost sixty, it is enough for dull guard duty. But he does not dislike it. Here, among the torch-lit corridors, he has enough leisure to indulge in the memories of days gone by.

Carefully he goes down the stairs, to a block whose cells are kept so low that even a small person like him could not stand up. If one wants to keep his body upright - only sitting, if one wants to stretch it - only lying down.

Slowly he passes the cells. Contrary to the rule, he glances only fleetingly through the small bars in the doors. Because his vivid imagination works already again and forces him to feel every possible sensation of this torture.

The tightness, the unbearable tightness. Fear of fire or water. Everything timeless, everything endless. He stops, looks back and forward again. »Here's the middle«, he says silently to himself, »now I'm already over the middle«, He walks on slowly. His fantasies are mixed with memories of prisoners of war, telling of this torture during his time in Sulla's army: ›How much longer? What if they never let you out of here? The cell seems to be shrinking. Impossible. And if it does, is it shrinking in height too? Straighten up quickly, no, it's not shrinking.... I'm no longer here... my body is dissol-ving ...I am no longer here.... No weight, I have no more weight...the body dissolves. Is that how being dead is, is that how it is when you're dead....‹ Nicodemus walks faster, almost running. Then drags himself up the steps until the view down into the block is closed by the curvature of the staircase. He sits down on the steep steps of the stairway to rest for a moment. He reaches for the scabbard, wants to pull out the sword in order to place it on his knuckles to cool them, because they hurt, as so often, but his hand reaches into nothing. He gasps, feels his heart beating under his chest. »Oh Gods«, he whimpers softly to himself, »don't do this to me.«

In the semi-darkness, he feels his way down the steps. Thick beads of sweat run down his forehead. In pain, he hurries back up the steps, trying hard to remember. *Where did I last use it, where did I leave it, where did I forget it.* Always tormented by the knowledge that he should actually sound the alarm, for Maecenas has already warned him: ›If anything else happens,

In case of further incidents, no matter what kind, you are you're fired‹ And there, sickness, poverty, death await. *No, no,*

he thinks, *I have to find it*. Suddenly it comes back to him, yet too late. The blade hits him in the heart.

Maecenas hurries through the corridors, orders a squad of guards to the great armoury as he passes, then rushes through the door, to his master's chambers, waiting neither for permission-giving facial expressions nor gestures, but releases his words like blows, each meant to pound in stakes. »There is commotion among the slaves! Several guards are dead! There are fights, fierce fights with our men!«

Batiatus asks no questions. They both run down the hallway and hurry up the stairs. At the top, they are almost overrun

by guards. One of the men grabs Batiatus' arm, a second one jumps, otherwise he would have fallen down. Batiatus gasps, beckons the captain to him. »What happened here!? Where did they get the weapons!?«

»No Idea, don't know. We found Nicodemus and some other guards, all dead. An armoury was broken into.«

»Wretched, drunken, worn down rabble«, Batiatus chokes out, »get out now, and I shall not hear the slightest sign of cowardice.«

For a moment he stares after those who hurry away before turning hastily to Maecenas again: »What about the guards on the towers?«, then, not waiting for an answer, »how many were able to leave their quarters?«

»I don't know.«

»Take care of that! Put all men on alert! Especially stones on the walls and towers. Spears only when absolutely necessary. I'll get reinforcements from town.«

Maecenas alerts the reserves, runs back then through the main tunnel to the nearest tower. At a crossing point, he stops briefly for he thinks he hears noise - roar of crowds quietly penetrating the walls. Arriving at the tower's ascent, he stops again. In Fact! Battle cries unmistakably penetrate from above. He unsheathes his sword and hurries up the steps.

Panting, he stands on the wall and looks down into the courtyard. A chill runs down his back. The gladiators seem to have thrown off their chains by the hundreds. Maecenas calls for one of the men, he yells to get over the noise:

»Hey! What is this here! What's going on here?«, He grabs and shakes him violently. A pointless question, a pointless action, but it helps release the initial tension.

»We need spears!«, the men replies with wide eyes, »we have to attack them with spears!«

Maecenas ' eyes fly along the Corona. Catapults are incessantly filled with stones, which arc down on the defenceless crowd. *Just relax, just relax*, he thinks. He has witnessed gladiator uprisings in other schools, but this is Capua, the greatest in the empire.

The yard is filled with thunderous noise of fighting, and what he sees makes him shudder again. Wielding a sword in each hand, a group of gladiators fights bitterly against the guards, who more and more often hide behind their man-high shields and retreat, seeking protection.

Maecenas works his way through the throng, looking for Burrus. »They're backing away!? What's going on down there!!!«, he shouts to Burrus when he finally knows him to be nearby.

»They're fighting with sharp weapons«, he replies panting. Rushed somehow, his voice broken, he continues, »I don't know how many there are, it's too dark.«

»Spears out!«, shouts Maecenas .

»If we go at them with spears, there won't be much left, and Batiatus said ...«

»Spears out, I say! I don't intend to impale them all, just scatter them. They won't withstand a rain of spears«,

and blows the horn himself. Fast, often trained speed, on the walls, in the corridors, in a flash, the weapon is pass out in thick bundles, first tips of the three-foot-long projectile hit their victims already. The clashing of swords breaks off abruptly. Sounds of pain and despair flood the walls of the school, seeking shelter the gladiators try to escape through the exits, but these are blocked by heavily armed guards. Exalted, Maecenas puts the horn back to his lips and signals to stop throwing. Then, turning to Burrus, »make sure the guards are still man the exits for about an hour. Don't mind the wounded gladiators, let the others see them - and hear them.« Leaving Burrus contentedly, he walks along the Corona towards the tower entrance. »Maecenas «, he suddenly hears Burrus' agitated voice and turns, more a reflex than out of concern, and follows his outstretched arm. A clew has formed from the sporadically gladiators running back and forth. From the gladiators, sporadically running back and forth, has formed a clew. One of the statues is overturn and immediately lifted up by dozens of arms. *For the sake of all the gods*! »Spears out, spears out«, shouts Maecenas to his men, his voice almost failing him. »They want to break down the east gate! Don't let them under the arch!«

The Centurions drive their legionnaires onto the walls closest to the gate. Stunned, with eyes wide open, Maecenas stares down into the yard, for the gladiators have taken up the spears, spinning them above their heads like windmills, protecting themselves and those who carry the colossus.

He looks again at the main tower. *There it is*, the sign of the approach of the reinforcements! Five hundred legionnaires are coming. Suddenly he is confused, hasty, notices the darkness. Angrily he calls for the guards to finally light the torches. Then, gesturing wildly with his arms, he motions for the tower guards to order the entire cohort outside the old east gate,

blows the horn again to stop throwing the spears, there is also nothing left to hit. The cohort should be able

to deal with the rest. Silence now, spellbound, the Romans look down at the vault of the eastern gate, but the darkness hardly reveals any details. Then, a cracking sound of bursting beams and splintering wood. Silence again.

Maecenas calls Burrus over to him. Both hurry down the steps, hurry through the corridor towards the exit. With trembling hands they release the lock and get outside. The torches are blinding, but they see twenty or thirty gladiators emerge through the broken gate and confront the vanguard of the cohort. And again, wielding a sword in each hand, with a speed as if even air were a resistance that must be cut, they bring the first onslaught of the vanguard to a halt, while more gladiators emerge behind them.

The core of the cohort comes closer, unmistakable the sound of double time. The gladiators, still fighting fiercely with the vanguard to help more of their own escape, gradually retreat, bow to their superiority and flee into the darkness. The cohort forms up. Forming a semicircle, shields in front, they surround the gate. Breathing heavily, at a safe distance, Maecenas waits to see what happens next, Burrus at his side. A moment of silence again - silent moments that want to become eternity. Suddenly, a dense swarm of spears shoots into the ranks of the legionnaires, tearing some of them to the ground or drilling into their shields.

Then the gladiators rush out and run against the crescent-shaped bulwark. Suddenly shouts of the legionnaires from the back rows. The gladiators, who have fled, seem to return and attack at different points, coming out of the darkness by surprise. But the Centurion of the cohort remains calm. Knowing the fighting strength and superiority of the weapons, he doubles the depth of the ranks and lets those behind turn to the outside.

Resigned, Maecenas watches the goings-on from a safe distance.

»Perhaps«, Burrus says, his voice betraying that he already knows the answer, »we should talk to the officers?«

»What for? It's too late for that now.«

At last, the fight is over. The legionnaires are still holding out in front of the gate, but it remains quiet. After the wounded are halfway treated and the dead counted, a courier is sent to inform Batiatus that the rebellion has been crushed, the leader dead, and about eighty gladiators have escaped.

Under the protection of two hundred heavily armed legionnaires, Batiatus returns the next day.

Once back at the school, he has Maecenas call out. »How many did we lose?«

»It's about five to six hundred.«

»What does Apulejus say? Can we cope?«

»I haven't spoken to him yet.«

»Any news of the fugitives?«, he continues to ask as he walks quickly through the courtyard entrance.

»They have withdrawn to Mount Vesuvius.«

»Withdrewn? One would think you were talking about an army.«

»Forgiveness, the events of the last few hours are still too present.«

Batiatus stops. Questioning, irritation, settles briefly on his face at Macänas' answer, then he walks on. »Among the men who escaped«, he turns back to him, »is there anyone we will particularly miss?«

»We haven't been able to make a list yet, but a Thracian named Spartacus is among them. He was one of those who fought in the house of Flavius. Survived the animal-baiting in the circus, was badly affected by the smoke poisoning, but recovered surprisingly quickly.«

»Pity about him. Once again! How many escaped?«

»About eighty.«

Batiatus reaches for the cloth, which is handed him and wipes the sweat from his brow. »They will surely send troops from Rome. It is not likely that there will be any survivors.«

Chapter 4.

Annaeus

Hortensius reaches for the woollen blanket and closes it tighter around his legs, for it's still quite chilly in the woods. Nevertheless, the path to the country estate of Annaeus Serenus is very pleasant. As a narrow path it flows through the woods, then over endless meadows, past lush vineyards and finally ends at a gentle hill, with the country house of his master.

He would gladly take more time, but he has only been in the service of Annaeus for a short time. His sober, coolly calculating manner had caught his eye. So Annaeus instructed his steward to entrust him with the errands to Rome in the future.

Senator Annaeus Serenus, half Samnite by birth, does not like flatterers for this service. Samnium was finally subjugated by Sulla ten years ago. Suspicion, distrust, disdain persists to this day. Nothing is more annoying to him than a courier who tries to gain trust by flattery, as if this feud did not exist between Romans and Samnites. News, good or bad, should be presented to him briefly and matter-of-factly. All circumlocutions and cautious insinuations are abhorrent to him.

Yet he is a Samnite only on his mother's side, his father comes from the patrician lineage. Thus, his country house is of lavish variety. A courtyard space with several fountains, is enclosed by a portico. This is provided with glass windows and protective roofs. Opposite, a dining room that projects to the coast. On all sides, swing doors or windows as high as the doors, and, depending on their location, give views of the sea, woodlands and distant mountains.

*

Annaeus adjusts his toga and scratches the back of his neck. This itch, will it never stop? He asks one of the slaves to bring him water. The woman fills a cup and Annaeus looks lasciviously at her hips. Greedily he drinks and makes himself over the exquisite meal.. His gaze continues to rest on the woman's body. *Perhaps still time to...? No! Hortensius could be here any moment.* A few moments later, he hears someone coming up the steps.

»Ave.«

»Feel welcome«, Annaeus replies impassively. Between two mouthfuls of goose liver, he continues: »Some slaves have escaped again, in Capua, from the school of Lentulus Batiatus. Is what I've heard so far.«

»He's in Rome«, Hortensius replies, »talking to some of the prefects and senators right now, wants reinforcements for his school.«

»Reinforcements!?« asks Annaeus crossly, lowering the arm he is about to use to shove a bite into his mouth.

»He's worried about the bunch that got away.«
Annaeus has lowered his gaze again and devotes himself to the dishes in front of him. »How many?«

»About eighty.«

»Do we have to deal with this?«, he continues without looking up.

»I say yes. We need trade within the country more than we would like. You know the Cilicians give us grain trouble.

Many traders will avoid coming as long as there is some gang of thieves hanging around Mount Vesuvius. So we should get rid of the problem as soon as possible.«

»Eighty—no more. Doesn't he have a few thousand in his school there?«

»Two or three thousand.«

»But only eighty escaped, you say?«

»It's said, there was a conspiracy, but it was betrayed.«

»Really? Look at this now«, Annaeus takes a deep sip from the mug. »All right. What' you suggest?«

»A cohort of six hundred men. Veterans who fought under Sulla. I think it won't be difficult to dig them out. Many of the army have degenerated into justly pitiable creatures, they will be happy to be soldiers again.«

»A whole cohort!? Not for this gang of butchers. It's only eighty, you said. We don't need six hundred men for that!«

»A cohort is easier to detach, a few hundred men...«

»Good, good, I see. Anything else I should know?«

»No.«

»But?« he keeps asking, noticing his hesitation as he continues to wolf down his meal.

»The slaves, you lent to your cousin to build the aqueducts...«

»Yes?'«, looking up from his plate with his trademark menacing look, as if he were going to scare the bad news that was about to come and get away before it hit him. But Hortensius is familiar with it. Undeterred, with the same tone in his voice, he continues: »There was an accident, some of them were squished.«

Annaeus' jaw drops, his lids widen. »By Jupiter most high, that was the last time«, he replies in a voice quivering with anger, and rises, faster than one would give his corpulence credit for.

»He will surely pay you for them.«

»How!? His debt mountain is higher than Vesuvius«, Annaeus retorts, completely beside himself, »a fool I was when I lent it to him«, and sits down again. With a sigh of exhaustion, he strokes his bulging doublet, beads of sweat stand on his forehead: »I'll cancel everything.«

»There are still four days until the celebrations«, Hortensius tries to change his mind, more out of a sense of duty than conviction, knowing that the cancellation will be lip service.

»No, it's no use. Now go and deliver my proposal to send a cohort!«, When Hortensius returns in the evening, Annaeus immediately calls him in and learns to his satisfaction that the Senate will send a cohort of six hundred legionnaires to Mount Vesuvius. It was also decided that Lentulus Batiatus would have to pay for the equipment.. ›After all, these gladiators are from his school‹ and, they went on to say: ›Through his carelessness they escaped.‹

»There you go«, Annaeus comments on the news, dismissing Hortensius for the day. He then walks once again through the rooms prepared for the upcoming triclinium.

Although he cannot find any negligence, he has one or the other work done again. *One must not give these creatures the feeling that they master their work.*

*

available

The orgies in the house of Annaeus are notorious. Already in the early evening hours the triclinium fills up with numerous guests. Stretched out on several slightly rising, crescent-shaped loungers, they take their meals with relish. Hour after hour, the most unusual dishes are served by beautifully built slaves girls: Dormouse flavoured with honey and poppy seeds, peacock eggs brushed with peppered egg yolk, plums dressed as coals stuffed with pomegranates. Piglets with red sausages spilling out of their backs, pigeons made of bacon, uteruses of young sows shaped into fish, stewed calves garnished with mutton kidneys. Fine wines low in streams. Interruptions are only necessary in case of compulsive relief of the stomach, but the person concerned only has to go to an adjoining room.

In one of the rooms that serve as a kitchen for this evening, Silana prepares the glasses with perfumed water. She checks the smell of each glass, pauses briefly and repeats the procedure again. The punishment is unimaginable if a bile-smelling brew were poured over the hands of one of the guests during the frequent ablutions. Opposite, on another shelf, the urination jars. Because even for the nature's call no one has to get up from his bed. By snapping fingers, slave girls can be summoned with an urination jar.

Silana examines her clothes, re-ties her belt and straightens her chest straps. At the age of ten she was sold into slavery.

Her femininity awoke early, by the time she was thirteen it was fully developed. As soon as this happened, the instruction followed, what purpose hip sway, kissing lips and voluptuous bosom are intended for. In the circles of Annaeus she was regarded as a creature particularly favoured by Isis, ›a really delicate ingredient in his orgies.‹

Cautiously, Silana walks to the edge of the atrium and listens to the scene in the triclinium. She takes in voices and moods. Reads behavioural patterns, recognizes characters from spoken words and their sentence melodies. As soon as she has to enter the orgy, she will draw from it, to evade the lustful desires of the guests for as long as possible.

The voices are cheerful, boastful. They know each other fleetingly, with few exceptions. They praise the cooking and praise the hospitality of the host. Attempting to relieve himself, standing at the threshold of the adjoining room, bent over, one of the guests loses his footing. Peals of laughter as the fattened, pot-bellied figure plops to the floor.

Slave girls rush in and help him into a more favourable position for emptying his stomach. »Hurry up«, someone calls across the room. »Here comes the next victim already.«

»Me too! Am about ready«, shouts another guest,

»By Zeus, I will not watch this feast of the palate pass me by.«

»Silana«, she suddenly hears Annaeus' deep and demanding voice, from the doorstep of the next room. She has waited too long, it is not good if he has to call for her. Without hesitation she rises. With quick but short steps, she approaches the triclinium, the voices growing louder, her soul writhing.

»Weren't you recently in the house of Tiberius?«, Silana recognizes the first voice, »tell us, how did it go there?«

»He is a model lout«, Silana recognizes another voice, »the guests are numerous, as can be surmise from his staus. But while he himself drinks the most delicious wine from Setia, he puts before his guests a sinister swill, the smell of which already causes nausea. To the point of serving them black-crusted bread, suspicious mushrooms, rotten apples.«

»An outrageous audacity!«

»But the most disgusting thing about him is the way he treats his slave girls.«

»You say it, my dear. He is hideously ugly himself, as you know. Reddish boils and bumps all over his body, including his face. The rage about his deformity he takes out on the slave girls, on whom he commits the most shameful acts. I myself have not a few slave girls and only recently I bought very young women from the Parthian Empire. They are of such beauty that I could not resist. Of course, they are with me to play the sweetest games. Granted, a little education is needed now and then, but the way Tiberius treats them is not worthy of a Roman.«

»How right you are! Give me some more of the veliter wine and let us drink to the beauty of our slave girls and that they may give us many more lovely hours.«

»Yeah, let's drink to that. Come here girl!«, Greedily he stretches out his arms. Silana just manages to find a footing so as not to fall entirely to the ground when an obese mass rolls down on her from above and buries her underneath.

Chapter 5.

Slaves

Emilius Lepidus owns some of the largest estates north of Rome, also calls two hundred slaves of the third generation his own. With the exception of the half-yearly grain deliveries, all the work is done by the slaves. From the mere cultivation of the fields, fertilizing, searching for stones, expanding the cultivated areas, creating and maintaining the irrigation systems, to the bone-crushing grinding of grain. The latter is considered a particularly severe punishment among his slaves, which Lepidus imposes for no reason. In this way, he says it himself, he keeps the fear of worse.

It is not uncommon for whole families to fall into slavery, and sometimes it happens that a son asks to take over the grinding for his old father, as is the case today. Lepidus has the father brought in, a frail appearance with an ice-grey beard.

»When the sun is at its zenith, you will relieve him«, he says authoritatively. Then, with an imperious gesture, he sets the slaves to work.

His horse is brought up to him. On shady paths he rides aimlessly across the fields, to be present, at uncertain hour and so to maintain fear. Fear of discovery of any carelessness. Thus, the day passes. At dusk, arriving his house, he is already expected.

»Forgive my late hour, honourable Emilius«, he is greeted by Lentulus Batiatus with due formality. »Circumstances delayed my departure.«

Lepidus, a grumpy man by nature, replies with a closed expression, »Be welcome«, and invites him into his house. The two men go into a cool, soberly furnished room. A slave woman brings a jug of water, along with the evening meal for her master. While she prepares the table, she asks Batiatus how he is and if he would also like a meal, but he refuses.

»It seems, the heat is troubeling you?«, he asks Lepidus instead, taking a sip from his cup before continuing, »I saw a dead man at the grain mill.«

»He was old, he would have perished in the fields within a week. At the mill it took half a day«, Lepidus replies.

»You don't take mules?«

»Mules cost 400 to 500 sesterces«, his strong jaws suddenly interrupting their efficient chewing work. Holding the spoon close to his mouth, he sends out a tough mass. »How's school going?«, he asks listlessly, eyes downcast, jaws chewing cud.

»I have lost many men. May their bodies go down the Styx to Tartarus«, Batiatus replies angrily, wiping the sweat from his brow. Lepidus gives him a look to express at least the appearance of sympathy, as he refills his cup. »Is there any news of the escapees at Vesuvius?«

»Hardly, -- they'll send a cohort.«

»A cohort? If so, there won't be much left of your slaves.«

»You're probably right about that. It's a real pity, especially among these are a few special pieces. There is a Thracian, tall, with a warlike appearance. By the highest Jupiter, never have I seen a fighter so skillful with a sword.«

»So? I've heard you say that before, in Rome.«

»Forgive me, my dearest friend. You see me somewhat saddened by the events of the last few weeks«, and pauses.

Sighing, shaking his head, he continues. »Oh, I wish I'd sold the school a year ago. What demon blinded me?«

Lepidus calls for the slave and has a jug of wine brought.

»You know«, he says after a while, »I always like to see you with me. You pay a good price, and when slaves aren't fit for the sword, I'm always the first you offer them to. But I can't sell you any of my slaves this year. A severe drought lies over the land. The hot days will continue, it means losses in the crops and losses in the slaves.« He waits for Batiatus to answer, but he sits in front of his cup with his head bowed slightly.

»I recently bought some new slave girls«, Lepidus continues.

»It's already night. You can stay if you want.«

Batiatus feels a hot greed rising.

Heavy knocking rouses them from their sleep the next morning.. the large, heavy entrance door of the house, but doesn't dare to open it. Lepidus, who rushes over, gives him a brief gesture to keep quiet. He beckons a slave to open the door. A young man, tied hand and foot stands in front of them, brought by Emelius' guards. »He tried to escape and killed one of our guards in the process. He is the son of the old man who perished at the mill yesterday.«

»Yes, I remember«, Lepidus looks at the dislocated shoulder and left arm, believing at first it's merely broken, realizing then the unnatural twist. The broken bones bulge and stretch the skin as if they want to pierce it instantly.

»Was that necessary?«, he asks them angrily.

»He couldn't be restrained.«

»The arm won't heal«, Batiatus says, noticing Lepidus' questioning look. »I have no use for him.«

»Take him in the fields and wheel him. Make sure as many of the others see what you're doing. I don't want any more refugee cripples paraded in the next few days.«

*

wildlife

Quintus Valerius adjusts his toga. The governor of Messina is coming through the gate, accompanied by his daughter.

»Welcome, Arius Victor, may the gods be with you and with your daughter. She is a true beauty.«

Arius does not respond to the friendly welcome. With a haughty frown, he looks around again and then turns to

Quintus. His way of speaking seems anxious and aggressive, worried and annoyed in equal measure. He is dominated by the need to express the difference between his own position and that of his counterpart with the pronunciation of each word. »Tell me! Is there cause for concern? I saw troops marching out of the city.«

»In Capua, a few slaves escaped from a gladiator school, yet we will soon have them.«

»Did you get my message?«

»Of course, Though I want you to judge for yourself, please.« Quintus leads his guests and their entourage through the eastern part of the city, past temples, through marketplaces, until they finally reach his house, where they are received by servants. He leads them to the terrace at the backside of the house, overlooking a lush garden. Under a shady canopy, he asks them to take a seat. Then he summons two slaves.

»The younger one is Iberian«, Quintus introduces him. »I've borrowed him many times. He is a true master of architecture.

Recently a slave gave birth to a son, he's his. I hope to use him the same way one day. The elder is Egyptian, certainly not as nimble, but his experience and knowledge are immeasurable. I bought him ten years ago in Judea, after he had completed a magnificent building for the governor there.«

Arius examines the slaves, feels them from head to toe. He grabs their cheeks, presses their lips apart, feels their arms, taps their torsos as he walks around them in a circle. »Not bad, what you're offering me! I'll buy the younger one.«

»Good, the younger one will last you longer, so you assume you understand that his price is higher. I won't sell his child and the woman, that goes with him, though.«

»Will he cause me problems if we remove him from his offspring?«

»It won't happen. Generally, they quickly come to terms with it. He won't give you any more trouble than a dog or any other creature.«

»Well, let's say four thousand sester...«, Arius' face tightens into a frightened grimace. He feels hands reaching out for him in search of support. Before he can fully grasp the situation, he sees the younger one fall to the ground next to him. Still dazed, he kicks at him: »By the gods, how dare he!«

»He must have fainted«, Quintus, keeping his composure, tries to save the situation.

»Why didn't you hold him?«, Arius shouts hysterically at the old man. »He understands what I'm saying, doesn't he!?«, yelling now at Quitus.

»Of course he does. He understands every word«, Quintus replies overly politely, anxious to soften the escalation.

Angrily, Arius tries again: »Why you didn't hold him!? Speak up, cursed brood of slaves!«

»Please, Arius, I am inconsolable this has happened to you in my house. I will sell him at half price.« With a slight movement of his head, he orders his servants to take care of the incident.

»Let's go over there«, he quickly speaks further, »I had the wine specially chilled.«

Arius already has the answer on his lips when his daughter's hands clasp his arm. »Let us think no more of it, father. We have always had pleasant days in Rome, when we have visited Quintus.«

»Yes«, he relents, »yes, you are right, my child.«

Relieved, Quintus instructs the old to leave, yet makes him understand taking care of the younger one, who seems to be coming around again. Then he devotes himself to his guests again, infinitely happy to know the daughter of this difficult, startled nature nearby.

The next morning, he gives his servants the necessary instructions to prepare for the departure of his guests. When they set off in the early afternoon and are about to pass

through the city gate, they are already awaited by an officer. »I greet you, Quintus Valerius, and also you, Arius Victor. Not knowing if I would still find you in your estate, I waited here to warn the governor of Messina and ask to stay temporarily in the city. The cohort, the six hundred men we sent out two weeks ago ...«, the officer seems to searches for the right words, »almost half of them are dead. It is also said that the number of recalcitrant slaves increases, considerably.«

»Recalcitrant slaves?« replies Arius, half questioning, half wondering. »I can't stay here, I have important business waiting for me in Sicily.« Tossing his head back and forth excitedly, looking from one to the other, he continues, »Are we already unsafe of our lives as soon as a few of these pets make off?«

»For the sake of your daughter, I ask you to postpone the departure. I am sure that tomorrow two or three cohorts will be sent to solve the problem.«

Arius wants to answer him, but his daughter holds him back:

»It's more than well, that I am with you father«, she says firmly. »Without me, you would surely set off.«

»Well, my child. It's certainly better if we stay here.« Then, turning to the servants accompanying him, »Well, you heard what I said! We are not leaving!« He wants to emphasize his words, but his attention is suddenly diverted, by the sound of a raeda, which just dashes in through the city gate.

»Who is this person?«, asks Arius, half to himself, half to Quintus. And his mind, just calmed, is now fully in turmoil again: »At the speed of an insane? Why don't the guards stop him? What kind of times are we living in?«

»Cornelius Serbius, a patrician«, Quintus answers and freezes at the same moment, hoping Arius will not hear the last word, whose gaze follows motionless Cornelius, until he disappears from sight at a crossroads. With a short head gesture, he indicates that he is now ready to return to the house.

Cornelius Serbius moves on with his entourage to the Forum to return some borrowed slave woman to their rightful possession. Ruthlessly he drives the wagons through the streets, who does not want to be run over, jumps aside.

Once at the forum, he stops and quickly climbs the steps to seek out the courts, when he is stopped by a Centurion. »What is it?« he asks in a jarring voice.

»Forgiveness«, the Centurion replies, »but the courts are closed.«

»Not today! Why!?«

»The Senate has assembled to deal with the slaves who have entrenched themselves at Vesuvius.«

»Still not done!?«, snaps Cornelius angrily. »Two weeks! Two weeks ago they sent the troops!«

»The slaves have crushed our cohort. Also, there are rumours...slaves are fleeing...occasionally ... from the lands in the area around Vesuvius.«

»Ha, by Zeus, what do you know. They should have sent legionnaires, not fattened recreational warriors.«

»They were battle-hardened men«, the Centurion replies meekly.

Cornelius wants to rip out his tongue, how dare he, yet cannot arbitrarily vent his rage on a Centurion, effortly he controls himself. »They were probably still dazed from the previous night's drinking binge.«

Whereupon the Centurion, cautiously, with an apologetic expression on his face, briefly raises his shoulders and lowers them again.

»Very well«, Cornelius then says, »let us wait until tomorrow then.« With the wild gesture of a madman, he makes the column turn around.

*

Comitium

Senator Annaeus walks up the steps to the Comitium. The hall is already filled, but he does not intend to expose himself to useless questions any longer than necessary:

Why only one cohort? Who commanded them? The mere idea of such kind of discussions makes him angry and furious at everything. Yet, despite all weariness, it seems necessary for him to be present today. An entire cohort was massacred. That sounded different from the report he heard three weeks ago of eighty escaped gladiators, hiding somewhere on the slopes of Mount Vesuvius. Something seemed to brewing there that should be contained as quickly as possible. On the measures, which one will decide today in the senate, he wants to influence as well as possible.

The Senate is a hive of activity. Eternal know-it-alls feel their hour has come, blame on all sides. Suggestions are made, discussed and rejected again. Gajus Cossinius is proposed to take command of three cohorts as general, but he declines.

»I'd rather resign my office than disgrace my name by going slave-hunting!«

Annaeus wants to intervene, but Cossinius continues,

»Besides, who are we to send three cohorts against shepherds and slaves.«

He discards his idea again, for he doesn't see a way to counter Cossinius' last objection.

The Praetor Gajus Clodius is finally assigned to go into the field against the slaves. He, too, is reluctant at first, but he is reminded of certain incidents in which he had greatly harmed the Republic, but had been treated with leniency by the Senate. Today is the day when it will be reclaimed.

*

Legionnaires

»Hortensius!«, Annaeus calls loudly as he passes the archway to his country estate, and again: »Hortensius!«

»I salute you«, and helps him off his horse. »I hope the hardships of the journey were worth it for you.«

»Oh shut up! Why must you always greet me with this gibberish!?« Sullenly he rejects the helping arms, allowing his sword and toga to be taken off, when suddenly he noticed the slaves and horses at the end of the colonnade. »Who owns the slaves? Do we have visitors?«

»Two of the merchants, nobles, recently guests of your triclinium, Publius Emelius Brutus and Antonius Dolobella.«

»What do they want!«

»They've come for the slaves who are wreaking havoc on Vesuvius.«

»Therefore?!« asks Annaeus sharply.

»That's what they told me, I didn't ask them.«

Annaeus leads both of them, with quick steps, through the inner courtyard, briefly eyeing the water features in which wall paintings are reflected. They will surely only smile at this, he thinks, and then calls to Helvia: »Bring us wine and olives, do you hear? To the atrium«, and asks his guests to make themselves comfortable on the seats. »So? What is there?«

»As we have learned«, Brutus begins with his usual formality, »the Senate intends to send two thousand legionnaires against the slaves to get hold of them.«

»And?«

»It was certainly difficult to find someone to take on this task, and Gaius Clodius deserves thanks for it. But he is basically not suited for it, you know that as well as I do. Therefore, we should give him three thousand men.«

»Nonsense«, replies Annaeus angrily. Brutus continues, but Annaeus barely listens. *I should have pressed Cossinius after all*, he thinks. Now, here, questioning the Senate's decision to these buffoons... »Have you lost your minds!«, he reproaches them. »We're not going to equip three thousand legionnaires just because a band of brigands is dwelling at Vesuvius. Three thousand men, that would almost be a legion! No! No way, -

besides, who says that Clodius isn't suitable? He has proven himself in war and has the blessing of the Senate! So?!«

»We have no doubt that also two thousand might be suffice«, concedes Dolobella. »We just want to be sure that this slavery problem is eliminated as soon as possible. We have difficulties with our houses in Rome because of Crassus. If now, on top of everything else, a gang of runaway slaves makes the area around Vesuvius unsafe, - Annaeus, I beg you. A thousand more men, no one will take offense. And in a week everything will be peaceful again.«

Annaeus puts an olive in his mouth and chews it slowly. »So, Crassus is the problem. Burned out houses that he has his slaves squads build. All right. But I won't achieve much empty-handed.«

»We can offer you a row of houses, close to the Baths of Helena«, Dolobella says hesitantly.

Annaeus takes a few steps to the end of the terrace. »I think three thousand would certainly be possible, and that will have to do. By the highest Jupiter, three thousand legionnaires, they can tear down Vesuvius and raise it up again.«

*

Rabble

Gajus Clodius is a middle-aged man and a member of one of the most important patrician families in Rome. Five months ago he was given the office of Praetor. The privileged status of his family did more than usual here.

Not only does he lack the necessary talent, but he also lacks the insight to leave such tasks to others. The polite distance, as well as the partly quite open ignorance of his brothers in office, left no effect on him. Yet the rejection of his person concerns only him as a civil servant. As a commander, in warlike
conflicts, no one ever found fault with him. During the civil war, he served as an officer in Sulla's army, was considered prudent and reliable.

When he was asked by the Senate to take command of the troops, he indignantly refused. ›Nothing but a disgrace‹, it immediately sounded among his annexes, ›to lead roman troops against slaves. A disgrace for the whole rank.‹ Only after further courting entreaties did he relent. Two days later, early in the morning, he went to the Mars-Field, where the troops would assemble, eager to watch them prepare and to become acquainted with the officers.

After an hour, he is more than shaken. »By all the gods. Is this the bunch we're leading to Vesuvius?«

The officers exchange a few glances. They are not surprised by the question. Finally, one answers him. »There is no lack of discipline among the men. It's, - we're marching against slaves. They are worse armed and their numbers are fewer than ours. The men know that. I think we shouldn't expect too much - in terms of discipline.«

»I concur«, says another officer. »But do not be alarmed, Praetor, the men are fully equipped. Each as befits a roman Legionary.«

Clodius wipes his eyes and forehead with his hand to hide the anger that is about to settle on his face. Then he gives his horse a gentle nudge and lets it trot slowly through the crowd. The officers follow him. Grumpily he continues to watch the hustle and bustle. Around noon the preparations are coming to an end, the last swords are oiled, lances are tied. Finally, he gives the signal to set off and the legionnaires arrange themselves into six cohorts.

Then it marches, the power of Rome. Unmistakably the dragging sound of chain-mail and breastplates. Clodius looks proudly from his steed along the rows, feasting the light storm of the flashing helmets. Were he campaigning against a 'real' enemy that day, he would leave the city through one of the main gates to the cheers of the masses, instead he leads three thousand legionnaires through the southern side gate.

On the fifth day they approach the massif of Vesuvius.

Clodius sends a scouting party ahead. After about three hours, they return and report that the slaves have set up camp on the high plateau: »That to which a narrow path forms the only access«, and that their number amounts to about a thousand.

He consults briefly with his officers. »We should take the opportunity«, is his final decision. Then he sends the scouting party ahead again, but lets his cohorts pause for an hour and then moves on with them. With the onset of dusk, they reach the designated spot at the foot of Vesuvius, where part of the scouting party is already waiting for them to report that the 'pack' is still camped on the plateau and that no encounters have taken place.

He listens attentively and exchanges ideas with his officers again. Then he speaks to the legionnaires: »This path is the only access to their camp. In order to supply them-selves, they must use this path. Either they attack us or they starve. I have no doubt that many of you are willing to march out and smash this insubordinate bunch to pieces. But why should we Romans bother to climb after them? All the way up to their camp and soil us with their blood? My scouts report there are about a thousand, encamped up there. We are of our three thousand. Means to me, they won't dare attack us. In a few days we will collect their starved bones.«

The legionnaires intone a shout of jubilation, striking their shields with their swords. Clodius raises his arm to return their cheers when one of the Centurions standing next to him asks:

»You really think they won't attack us?«

»They will attack us«, he replies, as he continues to receive the cheers of the legionnaires, »it's all what's left for them. But if we climb up, we lose our superiority in numbers.

Besides, there may be an avalanche of boulders waiting somewhere, or whatever else, by Zeus, they may think of.«

He thinks for a moment, eyeing path and landscape once more. »I want guards posted up to a distance of five hundred metres from our camp, along this path, checking each other over and over. I don't want this rabble to surprise us while we're stripping off our armor.«

*

are slaves

Sargon spent the last few days in seclusion, as so often happens when a matter with an uncertain outcome keeps him very busy. Outwardly he went about his daily tasks with his characteristic calm, but inwardly he was exceedingly tense. The first news from Clodius about the situation on Vesuvius should arrive today at the latest.

Contrary to his colleagues in office, he has doubts about the positive outcome of the venture. Early in the morning he sets off for the Servian Wall to hear first-hand about the success or failure of the Gajus. Once there, he briefly returns the guards' greeting, drives through the gate and place himself a little apart. It's very quiet this morning, just a few traders passing by. He wants to allow himself an hour of waiting, no more. The fog gradually disappears, the view stretches far down the Via Latina.

The sun rises and the stream of people coming up the road from the southern lands increases. He looks at the water meter, - *again today for nothing*, grabs the reins and lets his vehicle pass the gate again. As he passes, he glimpses an out-of-town beggar who is either completely disoriented or drunk

and staggers past the guards, who immediately take care of him and put him in chains.

Sargon hurries on to seek out the courts. Titus Aquicius, son of Sertorius, in his mid-twenties, well known to him, conducts the first trial. No judgement that is not in some way to the disadvantage of the less privileged class. He announces his decisions with a sadistic glee, feasting on the agony of the souls reflected in the faces of those affected.

Sexually disturbed, incapable, according to the women's stories about him. When Sargon enters the hall, the trial has already begun and one of the participants cautiously tries to persuade Aquicius to change his mind.

»I beg you to consider, five of his slaves witnessed the murder of his wife. Also, all the property of the murdered woman falls to the defendant.«

»But they are slaves«, Aquicius replies firmly. »They are not allowed to testify against their master, not even against their former master, that is the law. And therefore«, he rolls up the papyrus scrolls exceedingly carefully, »I see no other way than to acquit Septimus Optimus, who is here present, a respected citizen of our city.«

»The dagger, she was murdered with«, Aquicius suddenly hears a voice he knows. »Senator Sargon, - has something to object?«

»Septimus always carries it, which is known to any 'res-pec-ta-ble' citizen«, Sargon adds quickly. He doesn't think he'll overturn the verdict immediately, only stop it.

»That won't do...«, Aquicius breaks off abruptly and looks to the end of the hall, at the exit of which Annaeus suddenly appears.

»You are requested to proceed to the Comitium«, he speaks to the men without bothering with the usual greetings. »The guards have picked up a man, this morning, at the Servian wall, carrying news from Vesuvius.«

With the exception of Sargon, who knows how to hide his surprise, everyone looks at him with indignant faces. Aquicius senses that it is his turn to answer, as he is leading the negotiation. Visibly striving to speak authoritatively, he replies: »The matter has been entrusted to the Praetor Gaius Clodius«, pausing briefly, as if examining the melody of the sentence just spoken, »So why should we concern ourselves with it?«

»Because he's dead! That's why!«, Annaeus throws at him, »Gajus Clodius won't 'concern' himself with it.«

Sargon returns straight to his house, where Cato is already waiting for him. »They slaughtered the cohorts of Gaius Clodius.«

»I know«, Cato says. »What are you going to do now?«

»I will put on my robes and go to the Forum.«

»I'm coming with you.«

»You can accompany me, but you cannot attend the meeting«

»I'll have a look around.«

»Then come. Let's go, we're late.«

*

Only a few of the three thousand legionnaires have escaped. They must appear before the senate and answer.

»We had posted guards along the way, the only direction the slaves could come from. But then ... that morning they were suddenly there, out of nowhere.«

The Senate sends a cohort to recover the bodies, at least those of the patrician families.
In the semi-darkness they reach the deserted roman camp. Horrified, they remain on the ramparts until some of them break away to collect the corpses.

A detachment led by the Praetor Lucius Catiline makes its way up to the plateau. »Now let's go up there and see how those bastards got away.«
On horseback they reach the deserted camp, but can discover nothing except the rampart.

They pace the camp and finally stop at a steep rock face. Ladders hang on the wall, not recognizable at first glance. Ladders made of willow rods, artfully woven together, strong enough to carry the weight of several people. Silently they accept the answer they were looking for.

*

the ›Ego‹

»Their numbers are growing«, Sargon says dryly, as a greeting, as it were, when Annaeus finally appears in the side wing of the Comitium and sits down opposite him. He does the same as Sargon, who turns his right side to the table. Despite obesity, there is tension in Annaeus' posture, nothing to see from the man who foul-mouthedly devours his meals.

»It took you long, were you lost?«, continued Sargon, as dryly as he greeted him.

»Stop it! Shall I go again!«, retorts Annaeus. »There's hardly anyone here now, - I was expecting you outside!«

»I'll send a courier and we'll meet here, - don't know for how many years.«

»It's late, I don't have much time, an hour, no more«, Annaeus replies, with a short, rapid pronunciation to make it unmistakably clear that he has enough now.

»Their numbers are growing«, Sargon repeats bristly.

»The matter must be examined more closely. That's what they're going to talk about in the plenary session tomorrow. No one will want to be the first, who sees serious danger looming.«

»Where is Sertorius?« asks Sargon.

»Capri.«

»On Capri? That is, he knows nothing of the developments of the slave uprising?«

»No, he doen't know. But we shouldn't be so heretical as to speak of an uprising already.«

»When do you intend to call it an uprising?«, asks Sargon after a long pause. »After a talk with Dolobella and Brutus perhaps?« He doesn't intend to provoke him unnecessarily, though wants to put their meeting at the beginning. *From there it can go on*, he thinks, *there isn't much more.*

Annaeus doesn't make a face, hides in silence as if he wanted to let the question drain off him. »What I did when those two came to me«, he says at last, tilting his head as if seeking support, »is as common as the rain that falls on this city now and then, isn't it! - But above all - it wasn't me who chose that drip called Clodius!?«

»When they were with you, you spoke of him differently.« Annaeus replies with a shrug of his shoulders and the right corner of his mouth, made especially for such answers.

»If, what the few survivors say, is true«, Sargon continues,

»Clodius was better than ever. Or have you guessed they were weaving ladders, out of willow rods? Ever heard such a thing?«

»Why are you coming to me!?«, Annaeus asks annoyed,

»say what moves you tomorrow in the plenum, they will listen to you sooner than to me.«

»I would, if I had your years, came from the camp of the Optimates and the acquaintances from your orgies and drinking bouts«, Sargon replies, trying to tone down his bristly bass to soften his contradiction.

»What do you want me to do!?«, asks Annaeus, tightening his mien and leaning over the table. »Recommend sending five thousand legionnaires tomorrow, or even two legions? And how would I justify it...?«

»Same as meeting Dolobella and Brutus. It suited you, didn't it? You didn't give in because of the thermae, but because you don't believe in the nonsense of shepherds and herdsmen running to them.«

»That depends!«, Annaeus replies frostily and leans back demonstratively. »Don't think that you will move me to be the first to ennoble this 'insurrection' in any way, neither here, nor in plenary, nor anywhere else!«

Sargon bows his head slightly aside, indecisive whether to continue or end the conversation. »Samnites«, he finally says.

»What!?«, Annaeus rises angrily.

»Not even ten years have passed since the last fighting on roman soil, the wars, if you will, against the Samnites and Lucanians. That's what I see. How many fell into slavery back then, toiling in the mines or on country estates? That's where the influx comes from.«

Annaeus sits down again, not without a gesture of apology at his short-tempered behaviour. »Perhaps«, he then says, searching for words for his answer, »I am closer to you in your reflections than anyone else. But attitudes don't change that quickly, even if they had cut down five thousand. After the cohort didn't return, it was still a matter of putting things in order. I even wanted to press Cossinius. But then he said what can't have surprised even you. Here you see it again, - our 'mindset'. The gang at Vesuvius are no more than riffraff, some rabble, perhaps befuddled by some obscure religion that makes them think they can take on Mother Rome.«

»That's why I'm coming to you. That's why I speak of Samnites and Lucanians«, Sargon replies wearily.
Annaeus allows himself and him a break, even though he knows that Sargon would always reject such consideration.

»For the time being«, says Annaeus then, »there will be no one who will let words out of his mouth to ennoble this insurrection. What I did when they came to my house cannot be repeated, not now. Things will have to take their course. And then, necessities will decide, as always. And I don't think«, he adds firmly, »that enslaved Lucanians or Samnites will run towards them. But shepherds and herdsman! – And why not, these people know the area. Among the, - gladiators there will hardly be one who has ever seen anything but the school in Capua and the arena in Rome.«

»A thousand shepherds? In the area around Vesuvius?«, asks Sargon, formulating each word individually, thoughtfully, with a superficial appearance as if he's gradually beginning to believe it too.

»In public, that will be my attitude«, Annaeus relents. But then tries to give the conversation a different turn. »I spoke recently with your nephew, with Cato. He seems very fond, - of all that is taught in Alexandria. ›The 'I' is not absolute‹. Claimed by the brightest minds of our time. If they were in the Senate, they might say, ›be careful. These butchers may become warriors‹, yet they are not there. Enter the plenum tomorrow with such words and try to win over the senate, to make them see reason. Perhaps there will be 'only' laughter. And frankly, I too consider it, - no more than philosophical drivel that goes to one's head when the day is long. And as for Samnites and Lukans, - yes, not even ten years ago. But we were victorious. And those troops were not a hodgepodge of shepherds, herdsman, slaves, whatever.«

»They cut down three thousand, almost a whole legion...«

»They'll say it happens!«, Annaeus cuts him off. »The longer I listen to myself, the less I understand why you are so worried. Let their numbers grow, size makes fragile, if only for reasons of sustenance. Let them be two thousand tomorrow, and then? Where to go? What do they want to be?«

Sargon runs his hand over his toga as if there is something to wipe away. He senses Annaeus' waiting gaze and victory pose in his posture. »You remember the crucifixion of the four hundred?«, he asks him, as if casually, »happened perhaps a month before the outbreak in Capua.«

»I can't follow you!«, says Annaus.

»Whoever was born into slavery may be true for what a philosopher once wrote, for others...«

»Who!? Zeus, what are you talking about!?«, Annaeus asks irritably.

»You know his name, but it doesn't matter! It has entered our 'mindset', all our thinking, seeing, feeling. It makes us not only ...«

»Blind, but incapable, even where we can still see, you meant to say!?«, Annaeus interrupts him and starts a new question as Sargon does not answer. »What was with the four hundred?«

»One of them tried to kill the master«, Sargon speaks faster now, he wants to get to the end, he no longer believes he can make a difference today and hurls the sentences at him, like a list. »As the law requires, they were all crucified, outside of town, as always, along a road. Coincidentally, gladiators were brought back to Capua that day.«

»They saw everything. – Who was this one, out of the group of four hundred, who tried to kill? Was he just rabid like a dog? It will have been hate! Or have you never seen hatred in the eyes of your slaves? And now look to Vesuvius and add fear to hatred. Fear of the atrocities our world has to offer. – What is there, on Vesuvius? Is there someone who knows how to bundle this? That worries me.«

With an audible, peevish breath, Annaeus leans back again. He circles his head as if his neck hurts, but without taking his eyes off Sargon. »And if I agree with you now, what then? It won't change what was said! The forces that stand in the way of naming a danger will not disappear!«

With his crescent-shaped slits of vision, Sargon recognizes by facial expressions and gestures that for Annaeus the conversation ends here, Though doesn't wait for another word from him, but rises. Annaeu's tense expression about this behaviour is indifferent to him today. More and more often he feels the age, during such conversations. Ten years ago, he might not have accomplished anything either, yet wouldn't have let such a flow of words wash over him. Enough objections he had today too, but always foresaw the end.

»The Lanista from Capua, Batiatus, is here in Rome«, Sargon turns to Annaeus again after all.

»So? Why?«

»He's worried.«

»Fortune was with them, Sargon!«, Annaeus, for his part, once again takes the floor and uses the opportunity to rise, not to let Sargon go in this way. »Let's assume there would not have been such growths up there. The ladders made of willow rods block the view. Clodius didn't even have to chase these dolts up the mountain, they got themselves into this predicament. My point is - there is nothing special about their victory. They were lucky.«

»I don't think so! They didn't put themselves in an awkward position. They looked around up there beforehand. They expected Clodius to lay siege to them at the foot of Vesuvius, hoping to starve them out. As anyone else probably would have done. So the 'dolts' could strike, in dark night, from unexpected direction. - What does this mean for us? For the next weeks, months?« With these words he turns away and hurries through the exit of the hall.

Chapter 6.

Three Thousand

The day was unusually hot, not a breeze stirred. Even now, in the early evening, it is almost unbearable. Batiatus looks into the distance from his terrace, but a feeling of leisure does not want to set in. The events of the last few weeks have been too upsetting. A month ago he was the proud owner of the best gladiator school in the whole empire. Then the insurrection. Eight hundred were killed, including the leader. A loss that almost drove him to ruin. A small group of eighty gladiators set up camp on Mount Vesuvius and cut down six hundred men, who were supposed to clean up with this gang.

After that, they had a great influx, their number has grown to over a thousand. The Praetor was completely destroyed, a few days ago, at the foot of Vesuvius. *How long will it take for the remaining three thousand, to learn of this*?, it keeps nagging in him. *And then why shouldn't they try again to leave their hated cage? Or, worse, the insurgents themselves raid the school*?

He presented all this to the governor, with the request that about a thousand men should be given to guard him, also because the school was in a remote part of the city. One wants to see this ›rabble‹ only when one set them on each other in an arena.

The city fathers, however, did not share his opinion and thought it impertinent to bother them with this request. Times are bad, one cannot afford to hire a thousand mercenaries to guard a gladiator school. »Besides, we can't spare a man here.

We need the soldiers, that are available to us, inside the city. Rome has already taken care of this matter and will soon send new troops.« Until then, he should keep calm. »If you're afraid the rest of the herd will flee, go hire mercenaries. After all, it's your fault they managed to escape!«

In the end, he managed to persuade them to let him have at least one cohort.

*

Batiatus has reinforced the guard teams as best he can. Three or four of them stand in the towers of the walls and stare into the darkness of the night. The moon has set, the sky is overcast, the air is humid. Again and again the mercenaries run their hands over their foreheads as if wiping sweat from there.

»Keep eyes open!«

The mercenaries wince at the voice that so unexpectedly cuts through the silence that has lasted for hours.

The Centurion climbs the last rung of the tower ladder and stands with them. They all look ahead to the plain, but can see nothing except the mountain massif silhouetted against the horizon. Suddenly they think they see something. Something is crawling or wriggling on the ground, close in front of them, but it's already over! They all stare in the same direction, nobody says anything. It is up to the Centurion to sound the alarm, but he hesitates. The guard duty that has lasted for days has left its mark. Again and again they search the narrow, torch-lit ridge with their eyes – and there – there it is again, in a different place and there is another one...! For a split second they are paralyzed. Human figures slide across the floor along the torch-lit line, which they can trace with their eyes.

»By all the gods, it's them«, whispers one of the mercenaries, »they're coming, the insurgents.« The Centurion is about to call out into the courtyard - the guards on the neighbouring tower beat him to it.

Legionnaires are already rushing out of their quarters and form up around the walls of the school. Stones had been gathered days ago, as well as javelins, they are not unprepared, yet horrified to see a never-ending swarm of human figures approaching their bulwark, out of darkness at great speed.

The discipline of the roman legionnaires still holds. They throw their stones and javelins, overturn the ladders that, coming out of the darkness, are thrown against the walls again and again. But the enemy's numbers seem endless, pushes along the eastern side now too, like a stream that concentrates its forces before an obstacle in order to finally crush it. Panic breaks out in the ranks of the legionnaires.

Batiatus had already arranged for everything necessary to flee before the insurgents even reached the walls. No longer waiting to see how things will turn out, he leaves the school, driven by panic, with his confidants to go behind the safe walls of Capua.

From all sides now, the insurgents storm into the hated bulwark. Desperately, the Centurions try to regroup their troops and confront the enemy, their calls howl hoarsely through the thunderstorms of shields and swords.

Once again, for a brief moment, roman drill seems to triumph over fear, and they face the gladiators. But the unleashed demon of hate and anger is unstoppable.

Already the first mercenaries turn to flee, taking others with them. Yet many of them, unfamiliar with the school, its barracks, walls and houses, get lost, increasing their fear of death. Desperate and exhausted, sucking in the stuffy air, they rush through the labyrinth of stairs and corridors, calling for help. Death follows closely, chasing after them with strong, trained arms, sparing none.

*

Insurrection

Ruthlessly, Senator Sertorius makes his way through the turmoil on the Mars-Field. Tall, he overlooks the masses. His elbows mercilessly as soon as he thinks he sees which way he has to go. Finally, under an archway at the end of the Mars-Field, he recognizes the massive body of Sargon and pushes his way through the throng of people.

»Salve! I've been looking for you all morning!«

»So, why? Any special news?«, Sargon asks pointedly.

»Aaah, your nephew Cato, salve!«

»Sertorius«, Cato returns the greeting.

»There are rumours«, Sertorius goes on nervously, »they want to send both, Cossinius and Furius, into the field against the slavepack. We cannot agree to that.«

»No? What then? What should we do, I'm all ear.«

»What else should we do!?«, answers Sertorius in a bruised voice, »have you been standing here in the sun for long? Look at this rabble. They have been starving for months.

They might storm the grain stores or whatever else they can think of for gods sake. Shall we tell them that there is a danger out there that we are sending two armies against?«

»Tell him.«

Cato glances at him briefly, examining Setorius' facial expressions. »The slaves raided the gladiator school in Capua last night«, pauses, »two, possibly three thousand well-trained gladiators«

»By the gods«, nervously, breathing heavily, Sertorius grabs his forehead. »What is going on here? We almost sent out a legion, didn't we? Three thousand men?«, he hisses, temples pulsing with irascibility.

»That was two weeks ago«, replies Cato.
Sertorius looks questioningly, with his mouth half open, into the young man's face, as if he were telling him strange stories from the netherworld.

»And? Where are they now, these slaves who cut down our legionnaires? Do we still have legionnaires or are they just castrated lechers?«

»They have moved east«, replies Cato, »about to cross the Apennines. Scouting parties have been sent out to brief us regularly. The gate guards were instructed to turn away all traders and travelers by mid-day, they might have heard about it by now. After that, when admittance is allowed again, the message will probably spread within the city.«

»Moved on? Crossed the Apennines? Scouts?«, Sertorius is breathing heavily. »You speak as if we have an, - insurrection?«

Chapter 7.

Legions

For a year now, the insurgents have been holding their own in the centre of the world's power. Fear has spread through the country and is gradually penetrating the mighty walls of Rome. Shipments of grain are increasingly being hijacked by Cilician pirates, tumults on the Field of Mars when the Senate speaks to the people, and in the interior an army that roman legions have so far been no match for stands more fearsome and threatening than ever before.

*

Varinius

Sargon gets down awkwardly from the wagon and lets Jabulus know that he doesn't have to wait. With quick steps he aims for the Forum Romanum. Nothing urges him, but he wants to feign haste in order to get rid of tedious questioners.

Quickly he continues, the last meters along the Basilica Fulvia, then left into the narrow alley between the Basilica and the Comitium, here he waits, briefly listening to the hum that pushes through the alley from the Forum Square.

»Melancholy«, he mumbles to himself. »Oh, what do you want, I don't need you now.« He walks on, up the steps to the rostrum, the hum gets louder, as if from a beehive.

Once at the top, Annaeus, who had seen him coming, receives him. They both go to the right, then forward a little to survey the masses below.. To their left, Sertorius, who speaks from the middle of the rostrum, loudly, melodically, enunciating every word: »So far we've taken the insurgency lightly, but this time they're being met with the full force of our military machinery. You'll see, a few more weeks, maybe the next month, and then we'll be able to get hold of them.«

He raises his hand in greeting, grateful for the applause, which remains moderate, so he turns away, but gallantly, and motions for the herald to take his place to deal with all the 'nuisance' questions, all the nagging of this 'rabble'. Then he sees Sargon together with Annaeus, who greet him lightly.

With triumphant gestures he approaches them, tormenting in his neck the discussions of last night, his words, his thoughts, his reflections, which his brain ceaselessly repeats, hardly tamed, torturing him with other piercings: *Do they know about it? It should be. No, no...we would have... Shame oh shame. But it had to be... sweep away the rabble... but shame oh shame. So it's me, me, the first who has seen a danger in the slavepack.*

With angular, stiff movements, he finally stops in front of them, wanting to greet them, but Sargon forestalls him. »Salve, Sertorius. A successful announcement« and speaks so soberly and benevolently that even a Sertorius who is always looking for suspicion has nothing to complain about.

»Fifteen cohorts, three legions«, he says to them«, decreed by Aerarii Militaris.«

»Three legions«, Sargon repeats contentedly, approvingly. But he doesn't want to say more at first, because Sertorius' pronunciation, his lethargic, doubting tone of voice preoccupy him.

»As you requested«, Annaeus says to Sargon.

»Who is leading them?«, asks Sargon.

»Publius Varinius«, Sertorius answers.

»A procrastinator«, Annaeus agrees.

»That's what we call Quintus Fabius to this day«, says Sertorius emphatically, »who freed us from Hannibal.«

»Unanimous decreed?«, asks Sargon.

»If not, then!?«, asks Sertorius caustically.

»It seems to me«, Sargon goes on steadfastly, »you have come to your senses.«

»To what extent!?«, adds Sertorius immediately.

»After the three thousand we sent to Vesuvius, or the two armies, under Cossinius and ...«

»Will you lead them!«, Sertorius angrily blurts out.

Sargon does not reply, Sertorius' petulance sufficing him for the day.

»To what extent!?«, he, therefore, repeats sharply.

»You know.«

»No, Sargon. But, you say it!«

»Are they tools, Sertorius? Half human, unable to think clearly?«

»To me it's Pack! Lesser beings, and our legions will teach them what it means to rise up against us.«

»I hope so. For if not, no matter how noble the considerations of the roman order, they will be of no use to us.«

*

Varinius leads his legions in a northerly direction out of Rome, into the land of the Sabines, crosses the Apennines and advances further into Umbria, where the slave army

has been since early spring. That's where they went, two roman armies couldn't stop the advance.

Two days before Varinius reaches the area with his legions, he has Drusus, one of his officers, summoned to him. He has had many conversations with him, since they left, and believes to have found a reliable officer, even if he sometimes seems a little impetuous. »Choose a few men and ride to their camp. But I expressly ask you to avoid any risk of discovery. Send me word twice daily whether they remain there or break camp.«

Drusus chooses ten men and sets off. After five hours they have reached the area where they suspect the enemy to be and move only at a trot, avoiding any crossing of treeless plains.

On a remote estate they hope to get information about the insurgents. Their expectations are fulfilled. They are told to cross the forest in a westerly direction, after an hour they would be able to see the camp. Because of the horses, also for their own sake, they decide to take a short rest, then set off again and follow the hint.

As they reach the forest line, they put pads over the horses' hooves and lead them by the reins, even its slows them down, yet with the enemy close at hand, extreme caution is required.

At last the forest clears and indeed they recognize the camp in the distance, far enough away to avoid their detection, but close enough to see what they need to see. Sentries, clearly visible on the earthen ramparts surrounding the camp. In front of the mounds, deep trenches. One of these, it seems, is still being worked on. After a while they can even hear trombones, sure heralds of activities within a camp.

Drusus sends two of his legionnaires back to Varinius. With the rest of his men he crosses the forest to the eastern side, away from the enemy, to spend the night there. A decision that makes them ride late into the night, but should the horses become restless, it won't cause their discovery.

Around noon the next day, the two scouts return, inform him that Varinius is approaching and that they can leave the forest again to join him. Drusus asks no further questions, but gives the order to leave.

When they reach their legions, they are close enough to see the insurgent camp in the distance. Drusus lines up with his men near the Praetor.

The legions keep advancing, approaching the enemy camp until the guards on the enemy trenches lose their silhouette-like form.

Varinius summons Drusus. »Why isn't anything happening there?«, he asks him, looking straight ahead. »Possible he may not accept the battle immediately, but no one was to be seen on the earthen ramparts as we approached, except the guards.«

Drusus briefly glances at him, then looks forward again, his thoughts skimming over the scouting, but finding no hint of carelessness or possible false impressions. »It is as you say Praetor. I am equally konfused.«

Narrowing his eyes, Varinius continues to look towards the enemy camp. Licking his lips with his tongue, and with a strained thoughtful expression, he turns to Drusus again:

»Take some men and see what's going on there.«

»Praetor?«, he looks at him questioningly, hoping to change his mind about the danger of the plan.

»I said take some men and ride closer to the enemy camp!«, Varinius repeats firmly.

»Praetor?«, he looks at him questioningly, hoping to change his mind, for the plan is dangerous.

»I said take some men and ride closer to the enemy camp!«, Varinius repeats firmly.

Angered, Drusus turns away, grabs his horse's reins and sets off without answer, followed by three other men. They ride towards the camp at a light trot. Suddenly he pulls his horse back by the bridle and forces it to stand.

He feels heat, his heart beats faster, cold shivers on the back of his neck as he realizes the danger they are in. They ride back as fast as possible, Drusus stops close to the Praetor.

»And?«, he asks, »speak up!«

»There is no one there, the guards are dead men whom they have tied to poles.«

»But you passed to me words about trombones, that large detachments on horseback left the camp and came back!«

»It happened exactly as I sent word«, Drusus replies, recognizing the horror on the Praetor's face. *For all the gods' sake, he must give the order.*

But Varinius looks around him, looks over his legions, the sudden murmur - not to be missed, the movements within the cohorts - not to be overlooked. »Praetor! The troops must form up!«

Varinius feels Drusus' grip on his arm. He looks to the camp, then to the western horizon, then back to Drusus' face, who at that moment sees the enemy at their back.

No longer waiting for the Praetor to raise his voice, he shouts into the ranks of the legionnaires: »Enemy at your back!«, commanding the Centurions with his arms at the same time.

The turning of the troops is quickly executed, yet the arrangement of the legions is inevitably to their disadvantage. Already the enemy storms in and falls upon the five cohorts who stood back as reserves and must now be the first to face the enemy.

Drusus rides along the battle line and whips the legionnaires forward, turns his horse again, riding in the opposite direction, when suddenly a new shock runs through his limbs again, - the main force of the enemy has just appeared from the north-west, only a few miles away, and he must realize that they are lost, yet calls for the legates, orders them to withdraw two-thirds of the cohorts from the eastern wing and core to set them up in a new battle formation. Fine dust, whirled up from the ground, mingles with the combatants. Desperate, Drusus realizes this further disadvantage, *they see clearly how we stand, while we can hardly recognize each other.*

The north-western main force is approaching, fast, without noise, without shouting, nothing can be heard except the clanking of armor, mixed with the dull sound of thousands of people running across the ground. *Why aren't they roaring?,* Drusus thinks. *Why aren't they shouting, - anything?*

The legionnaires shouting their 'bara', beating their shields in encouragement. Then the first units clash. Dust shrouds the battle line here as well. Then, noise, voices, and sounds penetrating through, take away Drusus' last hope.

He spurs his horse again. Where is the Praetor? It is now his task to protect him. In a hollow, whimpering, half buried, he finds him, - his face covered in dust, barely recognizable. Drusus and his faithful do not ask any questions, they grab the Praetor, put him on a horse and ride on with him, looking around again and again, feverishly seeking orientation, but there are only veils of dust passing by, roaring the battle from all directions.

With great effort, pursued again and again by enemy cavalry, they manage to escape. *What a shame, when have roman legionnaires ever had to flee from slaves.*

Chapter 8.

Cilicians

The man takes a few steps to the bow and stands at the railing. He glances into the night sky, as he often does at this hour. The air goes calm, smooth the endless sea, sliced by the ship's keel. Darkly, on the horizon, can be seen the coast. There, somewhere beyond the darkness, the rebels are waiting, for them, the Cilicians.

»They say the insurgent army has split up, while advancing north.«

The man on the railing turns around, slightly frightened by the sudden voice, for no one but him was on deck. He waits for the man to emerge from the shadow of the sail, and turns his gaze back to the sea. The other one places himself next to him.

»Why?«, the man standing on the railing asks after a while. The other does not respond immediately, perhaps out of partiality before the events, perhaps out of awe of darkness and silence.

»Supply, time«, he answers half-loudly. »They want to cross the Alps, they say, before the onset of winter. One of the consuls. . . «

»One of?«

»Rome sent both Gellius and Lentulus, - after Praetor Varinius was defeated. They met the part that was marching further west. They say they're all dead. They were mainly Teutons and Gauls, and the leader, Crixus, a friend of the Thracian, was also said to have fallen.«

Both keep their eyes straight out to sea, occasionally glancing up in the night sky as if there were something new to see.

»Are you worried that they might not come?«

»They will.«

»How many meetings have there been - with them?«

»Three, today the fourth. - After the first, no one believed there would be a second.«

The man standing at the railing reaches for a wood carving from last night, left unfinished between the ropes.

»What's on the list?«, he asks the other as he draws the dagger and attempts a few cuts. The other briefly watches on the nervous, carving fingers, trying to complete the work.

»Three hundred talents are required. In return they get helmets, armor, lances, also ores and tools, - everything needed to manufacture weapons.«

The other puts the carving back between the ropes, as he doesn't want to succeed after all. »Maybe the last time we deliver them war equipment?«

»Possible. They are still fighting with the two consuls.«

»Still fighting?«

»Gauls and Teutons who marched further west were not the largest part, perhaps twenty thousand, they say. Then, after the first battle against the Thracians, the consuls fled almost as far as Rome. He pursued them, then swerved east, toward the Adriatic coast, and then north again. The consuls probably guessed what he was up to, took good passes over the Apennines, cut off his path, - the rest is still too imprecise. There were several battles. Some say he followed the Romans too far, led by grief, pain, vindictiveness, because of the fallen

Gaul, the Crixus. And thus lost the chance to reach the Alps in time.«

»Good for us. If they beat the consuls and do not come over the Alps, they will turn back. And who but we could supply them.« He glances up in the night sky again and sees what he has been waiting for hours. »Today, it has to be quick. They have the enemy in close proximity, - at least probably. We shall not set up camp for the night either, - back to sea as soon as possible« With these words he turns away, for they are approaching the coast.

The oars hit evenly into the water, the shore clearly visible. The Cilicians have the moon in front of them, they must already be clearly visible to the insurgents, while they only see shadows moving slowly along the shore, to get to the bay where the boats will stop. The pirates estimate their number at five to six hundred, plus another two hundred on horseback. Some are making bets as to which of the Thracians will be there. Yet no one believes they will get to see him. ›Why should he make himself known at such meetings?‹

The boats stop in a long line along the embankment. The captain communicates briefly with one of the men on the bank, everything else is routine. The boats are quickly unloaded. Hardly anyone speaks. The air breathes distrust, on both sides. After two hours the boats are unloaded and the insurgents are on their way back, as are the pirates.

*

his Wife

»We must send reinforcements to the garrisons in the north«, comes the energetic demand from the ranks of the nobility.

»Will you stand before the people tomorrow and speak!?« retorts one of the senators sharply. But the nobles get encouragement from one of their fellow officials. »Six legions we had placed under the command of the two consuls. Two have returned ...«

»Enough! We heard it!«, Sertorius cuts them both off and gets up angrily. »And you«, he snaps at the nobility, »dare to withdraw your belongings from the northern estates. We're doing our best to keep the mob in check when suddenly you appear on the northern streets, sowing fear and cowardice among the people. Shame on you.«

»Then do something to contain this rebellion. Fifty thousand warriors are with the Thracian, and no one knows whether there will be sixty thousand tomorrow, or, or, or turning his army for marching south again!«

»Or!? What else!?«, Sertorius interrupts him in a rage, »you should hear yourselves talk! Warriors' Thracians, army!«

»Perhaps it's time to put this threat in a more suitable tone«, Dolobella remarks in a cautious inflexion.

»No, I don't think so!«, rages Sertorius further, »there is no army! Neither warriors, only slaves! Beware of using euphemisms. Once you start doing so, they will also come out your mouth' in your speeches to the people.«

»By Zeus, then they hear it«, Annaeus replies. »The Thracian is about to wear out the whole Po-Plain, he is trying to break through by any means., he is trying to break through by all means necessary. Who gives a damn about the speeches on the Mars field?«

»How dare you, wretched Samnite ...«

»Stop this nonsense!«, they are interrupted by Sargon's rumbling bass. »Now is not the time to take up age-old feuds.«

»Certainly not«, Sertorius retorts demandingly, turning to him. »I have already missed your objections, Exalted-One. Have you nothing to say?«, he asks with effervescent sarcasm.

Sargon waits with his answer until all eyes have turned to him, thus declaring Sertorius' sarcasm a nullity.

»Cassius stand ready. He can lead four legions out of the city as early as tomorrow and reinforce the garrisons in the north.

»Cassius stands ready?«, asks Sertorius in surprise. »Without consulting us?«

»There are already assaults on the population, it seemed appropriate ...«

»Assaults? Of what kind?«

»Welll, - there are slaves there too, - in the cities, the estates. Slaves who fight against us in the Thracian army are looking for kin there.«

Sertorius crosses his arms. Hiding embarrassment, he glances around, out of the corner of his eye. A deeply human behaviour on the part of the slaves, which one must take note of for tactical reasons.

»Listen to me!«, he says after a while, which everyone has passed in silence, finding his way back to his authoritarian way of speaking: »Here is what we should try. This Spartacus was captured during the campaign in Thrace. In his homeland.

What happened to the families, the women and children? Did he have a wife? If we find her, we'll get to him, too.«

»There are about fifty thousand slaves who have joined him. Impossible, that he alone commands them all«, one of the senators points out.

»Rumour speaks of a Gaul named Crixus«, a noble interjects cautiously, »this one, be leader, alongside the Thracian.«

»Are you still among us!«, Sertorius sneers at him. »Dead, rotting already. Along with the twenty thousand who followed him. Only, alas, that was already the end of success. And even this, no triumph of martial prowess of our troops or art of war of our two, two consuls!« With a dismissive wave of his hand, he continues. »Let's focus on facts. Among all these slaves running towards him, there are also many who were born into slavery. Slaves who have known nothing but to follow their master. Who saw it as their destiny to be slaves. Suddenly they have a sword in their hand and think they can kill us all and then live in freedom? Oh no! They believe it because someone tells them to. They believe it because this Thracian, in whatever way, makes them believe they are people who have the right to be free. If ever there was a situation to cut off the head of the enemy force, in order to get rid of him, it is here.« Pleased with the successful speech, he raises his head but keeps his expression serious. No gesture, no emotion, lets leak out his relief. His most important mark for this day seems to have been achieved. Keep calm! Show strength! No one may outrank him. Especially not in upheaval times by rebellious slaves.

»Exceedingly profound thoughts, which we ascribe to a savage, a barbarian«, interjects Sargon cynically.

Sertorius strokes his toga thoughtfully and replies in slow, drawn-out words: »My dear, my thoughts are solely directed towards the safety of Rome. And if, in the process, I have to temporarily believe that a former gladiator, a slave, can bewitch whole armies of slaves, thanks to a mystical power, it's fine with me. But don't worry. As soon as this upheaval collapses, my conception of the world will move back to the old, familiar tracks. How about yours?«

»It will also move in the old, familiar ways.«

»Well, it seems to me that peace has already returned halfway.«

A servant of Sertorius enters the hall, whom he immediately beckons to him: »The merchant from Athens has been waiting for an audience, for several days«, the servant lets him know. Sertorius Mine darkens. Unintentionally, evil looks flee his face, roaming the hall as if he were looking for a suspect. »Tell him to be patient for another day or two«, Sertorius replies, arranging his countenance.

»I ask forgiveness, but he already seemed very irritable because of the lost days.«

Sertorius rises. He tugs awkwardly at his supposedly ill-fitting toga. These merchants. May Zeus wipe them from the earth with his lightning. Then he speaks to his servant again:

»Ask him anyway, beg him if you must. The last thing we need is the mockery of the Athenians.«

The servant bows and leaves the room.

»Any further questions, thoughts on the matter?«, asks Sertorius as his body slaves put on his robe.

»There are still the Cilicians«, the nobility dares an objection after all: »It's only a rumour, but... the slaves would have paid them four hundred talents, it's said, four hundred. And they want to pay that much again as soon as the ships are handed over to them. In case the escape across the Alps fails.«

»Believe me, this is completely irrelevant«, Sertorius replies, motion his slaves and mounts his sedan chair.

»Believe me, it's completely irrelevant«, replies Sertorius, giving his slaves a hint, whereupon they help him into his sedan chair.

»Be so kind and let us share, in the causes of the irrelevance.«

»Of course, you poor fools. Where would the Cilicians take them? Delos!? Where they themselves sell hundreds and thousands of slaves? Oh, no!«

They will surely continue to supply them with weapons and ores, but they will not create an army of slaves out of the country against which they would then have to fight them-selves. They will help to keep them here.« At the exit of the hall, waiting for the wings to open, looking out of the sedan chair, he speaks to them once more: »And I believe the slavepack themselves know this, too. But they'll be clutching at that straw, that might still be useful in one way or another.«

Sargon leaves the Comitium, only a little later after Sertorius. Dusk is already falling, but the full moon shines bright and clear as it rarely does at this time of year. Hastily he descends the steps.

»Ave, Exalted One«, he hears an unfamiliar voice. Turning towards it, he recognizes three men on horseback between the arcades.

»Please forgive us for appearing so suddenly at your back. We have waited for you here in this place, brightly lit by the moon, so that you may see us at once. Since you didn't, I had to call out to you.«

Sargon eyes the stranger. Jet-black hair, underneath an elongated face with a pointed chin. His companions wear helmets whose protection covers their noses and cheeks.

»I am Thrajan of Aquinas«, the stranger continues, speaking with a polite detachment that demanded respect, as those often do whose tone sounds, unintentionally, petulant and dismissive. »One of the nobles from the northern provinces sent to Rome to hear your thoughts, your plans, about the situation.«

»I remember. You were at the trial«, Sargon says.

»Yes, we were.«

»Is there any particular reason for your attendance?«

»It seems appropriate to me to present my thoughts on containing the insurrection to a single senator, lest they be drowned in the waves of the assembly.«

Sargon wants to ask why they are seeking him out with their request, but he pushes the question aside as too idle, they may have their reasons. »All right, I understand. Let's hear what moves you.«

»Someone spoke of a woman, his wife, and that she must be found.«

»And?«

»I think he himself is already looking for her, this will be the reason.«

»For what?«

»The force of the attacks«, Thrajan answers shortly.

»That bad?«

»Yes! Besides, – he's trying to break through, by all means. For he will not try to cross the Alps in the snow, they are then impassable. And he knows this himself. He would have to move south again just to resupply his troops, which will be more difficult than when he advanced.«

»Yes! Besides, – he's trying to break through, by any means necessary. For he will not try to cross the Alps in the snow, they are then impassable, which he knows himself. He would have to move south again, if only to supply his troops. Which will be more difficult as it was when he advanced.«

Sargon moves his head slightly in an understanding gesture. He senses that Thrajan is only trying to assess him so far.

»It's no longer just gladiators and mine slaves he frees or who run to him himself«, Thrajan continues. »They are master builders, scholars who were still teaching our children yesterday. You understand? Under no circumstances may the Thracian cross the Po plain. If he succeeds, the insurrection will take on an unimaginable dimension. And by no means do I just mean the concern of what an army of insurgents could unleash beyond the Alps. What about the Latin tribes? The Umberians, Sabines, Senones, Etruscans, will they not try again to free themselves from Roman subjection? And by this, I don't at all mean only the concern of what an army of insurgents could unleash beyond the Alps. What about the Latin tribes? The Umberians, Sabines, Senones, Etruscans, will they not try again to free themselves from Roman subjugation? We need reinforcements, more than just a few legions. Even if we don't take him down, it would still be an advantage. Like I said, he'll have to move south again.«

»I understand«, Sargon says, realizing that Thrajan is waiting for an answer. »Yet I see no reason why you didn't want to state this during the trial.«

»With all due respect, Senator! Hardly a word on the cause of the victory over the Gaulish-Teutonic heap. When Sertorius diminished the triumph, anger and rage were his companions, otherwise these words would not have passed his lips. Other speakers seemed more concerned with reputation than with the actual situation. Speeches for the common people, the Mars-Field, one's own goods. On the way here, we didn't encounter the ›people‹. The streets were empty, the cities gloomy. Fear has settled over the land, but it is certainly not our escorts who now and then escort our belongings to safe climes. They fear the army of slaves, led by a Thracian named Spartacus, who leads them against our legions as if the gods themselves had taught him the craft of war. And war craft, as you certainly know, means more than leading men into battle. They must believe, must be provided, must be, must be. And in his case, - all this in an unknown land, against an enemy with whom it is well known.«

»It surprises me, to hear someone from the nobility speak like that, - about the rebellion«, Sargon replies with a slightly doubtful tone.

»It is no more than a rational reflection. Perhaps you may agree now, why I thought it might better not to speak in the Senate itself. I thank you for the audience. This was our only request. We will now set out on the way back. May the gods be with you.«

»May the Dioscurs accompany you on your journey. « Sargon looks after the riders when he suddenly hears Cato's voice behind him.

»I didn't mean to startle you or to eavesdrop on you. I came at the appointed hour to pick you up. I could hear you before I saw you. It has seemed you both are in a quarrel, so I came closer. But it wasn't, so I kept staying behind.«

»Never mind, pack it in, it doesn't matter what you heard. Let's go.«

Together they walk across the moonlit square, heading for the steps that lead down to the Curia, their long shadows hurrying ahead. »Was our conversation so boring?«, asks Sargon as they reach the steps.

»No - but it may wait till tomorrow, you need rest.«

»Nonsense!«, says Sargon in a good-natured rasping voice, »what's on your mind? I'll sleep better and so will you.«

»Have you ever seen Thrajan before, or heard of him?«

»No. You were surprised, - weren't you? As am I, to hear him speak thus?«

»Yes, - I was«, Cato admits, suspecting that Sargon wants to hear more about it, but his thoughts revolve around other things: »Thrajan spoke of Sertorius and that he said too little to cause the victory over the Gauls.«

»You think we didn't win? Not really?«

»I still have Thrajan in my ear as he spoke of it, it didn't sound like...«

»My dear, one would think you hoped and wished they might make it, over the Alps.«

»You don't?«, asks Cato straightforwardly. Sargon turns around, for Cato got a little behind. Both look at each other, and just as Cato knows that he can open such thinking only to him, Sargon knows that it is only the years that make him think differently. »I hope there will be a world without slaves, at one day. Yet I don't want our world, our culture and science, to be swept away in a firestorm. And that is precisely what I'm afraid of.«

»So it was not a victory - of our consuls - over the Gauls?«

Sargon reaches for his arm, »help me«, he asks him. Cato helps him onto the raeda, while keeping an eye on the horses. Then he sees the exhaustion in Sargon's face and instantly regrets not having urged him more vigorously to wait until tomorrow.

»We have cards«, Sargon continues unexpectedly, »even cards that only exist for us. The insurgents – hardly. So our consuls knew they could catch up with them and did, forced it when they learned of the separation. – A valley in the shape of a funnel became the doom of the Gauls. – Separation, to reach the Alps faster, – basically the right thing, already because of the length of the marching column. Still, with maps only approximately good as ours, they wouldn't have done it, not there.«

*

In the shallow waters of his thermal baths, Sertorius enjoys the benefits of his slave women when Lucanus appears for the second time. Depressed, as it were filled with melan-choly, he climbs out of the basin and lets himself be rubbed dry by his slaves.

»What is it?«, he asks lethargically as one of his house slaves reminds him again of tonight's commitments.

»Gajus Pulcher requests an audience. He has been waiting for you for an hour.«

»He'll have to be patient a little longer. Out!«, Sertorius puts on his tunic and strokes the purple stripe, glancing again and again at the gold ring on his hand, which his father wore already. The ring and the purple stripe, the two symbols that mark the Senate rank. That he himself would one day be a senator was as certain to him as the gold content of the ring. There are Gods, there are Rome and its senators and there are slaves. Rules, order, that wants to be in this world, which he believes in. *No coincidence, certainly no coincidence, that we are destined to rule over others.* All his doubts seem to be gone, final, as if they had never existed. *They are born to serve, that's what they are good for, that's where their place is. Our arts, our writings, our sciences bring light to the world. This rabble knows nothing of all this. They should be thankful to be part of it.* Filled with these thoughts, he throws on his toga and leaves the thermal baths to devote himself to Pulcher. Without greeting, he approaches him. »Let's hear, what is it, what is so urgent that you must disturb my bathing?«

»We need legionnaires for our protection, at least a cohort.«

»Impossible!«

»As the rebellion grows stronger, more and more bands of thieves and robbers join together to form large troops that threaten our lands.«

»Why do you come to me with this!«

»You are the Praefectus Aerarii Militaris. Who else would I go to!«, Pulcher upset retorts. »We need more protection if ...«

»I can't deploy troops to protect you, they're marching north!«, Sertorius snaps. »Where's your patriotism!? Take up a sword and fight the pack yourself, - or do you lack the courage? If so, my dear friend, collect the belongings from your estates and take them behind the walls of Rome. That's what I can offer you. That's the situation we're in«, and meets Pulchers horrified eyes for a moment. »But if you have any idea how we can get rid of the rabble, speak up!«

»You forget with whom...«

»No! You've forgotten who you're talking to, now get out!« With a vulgar gesture, Pulcher throws back his toga and leaves the room without greeting.

Sertorius remains alone. *Thieves-Gangs, Rabble-Bands, of course these are coming now too.* The sublime attitude to life that has just returned seems to be dissolving again.

Oh Gods, let it be over soon, he implores in his thoughts. *I want to walk in my gardens again, listen to the flute, offer sacrifices for your pleasure.* He succumbs completely to melancholy and self-pity. *Sargon will speak to the legionnaire. I will ask him politely, and he will do it. I can't, by the gods, I can't.* Then suddenly, filled with fear that he might be seen like this, he scolds himself a fool and talks to himself in all sorts of ways, till he remembers the hearing in the Curia and calls to Lucanus: »Let the carriage be ready, I must go to the Curia, it may be late.«

»As requestte.«

Sertorius enters the Curia last, greets Annaeus and Sargon, three other officials who, for their part, are cautious. Although the hearing is public, only two representatives of the nobility attended, Cornelius Serbius and Antonius Dolobella. But none of the senators want to ask what made them attend. The occasion weighs heavily, they wait tensely for the curio to

announce the man they have gathered for. Eventually, he enters the room and announces that a legionnaire is waiting outside the door, insisting on being let in.

All eyes turn to the door. A young man, no older than twenty-five, enters the hall, looking around questioningly. No one had told him why they wanted him here at this hour. Slowly, but without hesitation, he approaches the group of senators.

»What type of manners are these?«, roars Cornelius in the legionnaire's face with his pricking voice. The young man flinches briefly, then freezes in a military stance.

»Shut up«, Sargon growls in his piercing bass. »We are not here to waste our time with incidental lapses of military discipline.«

»He's one of our legionnaires, and he owes us respect«, snaps Cornelius.

»Your nobility is of no importance here. I advise you to submit! Or by the gods, I'll have you thrown out!« Sargon's narrow slits meet his eyes, making sure that the screamer will finally give peace.

»Come closer son, there is nothing to fear«, he turns reassuringly to the legionary. »We have sent for you because we have learned that you may have been present at the capture of Spartacus, about two years ago, under Marcus Glabrus.«

»Yes, I was there.«

»Well, tell of it, let's hear, might be intresting?«, says Sargon.

»We caught him in the enemy camp, outside one of the tents.«

»In the enemy camp? Does that mean he escaped and abandoned his people?«, Sargon asks further.

»No. He fled only after everyone else ran away too, after the last resistance had collapsed. We gave chase.«

»In full armor?«

»Yes. We were sure he was too exhausted to escape us.«

»Why didn't you kill him?«

»We would have done so, if only because he himself sought battle, but on the orders of the Centurions we let him live.« Sargon takes a deep breath and exchanges a glance with Sertorius.

»How did you know«, Sargon keeps asking »that it was him, the Thracian, Spartacus, whom you followed?«

»We didn't. Late at night we reached our camp with him as a prisoner and brought him to the others. While doing so, we heard his name several times. There were no joyful exclamations, no shouts of joy. They all spoke very softly, only in whispers, but I have no doubt, Spartacus is the name of the man we brought into our camp that night as a prisoner.«

Sargon touches the group with his narrow slits, embarrassed silence spreads. »The reason we asked you here«, he continues, »and why it's so important to know if you really got that close to him, - maybe he had a wife? Possibly she, too, fell into captivity?«

»He had a wife. But she is dead. He himself killed her.«

»That barbarian«, Cornelius interjects, intent on rejoining the senators. »He killed his wife. Why on earth did he do it?«, looking down at the ground questioningly, and shaking his head.

»To make sure our legionnaires can't rampage over her, dunce!«, is Sargon's angry reply, »conversation is over!«

»Not so fast!«, Sertorius holds him and the others back.

»Where is Marcus Glabrus? Perhaps we should put troops under his command? He brought that creature here! Was successful with his campaign in Thrace! Did I listen correctly? Correct me, if not! The next troops we arm should have him as commander.«

»That might be difficult«, Sargon replies, »we exposed him in front of everyone for trifles. You remember?«

»No, not at all. Should I?«, asks Sertorius. »I think you would be just the right man to take care of him.«

»Glabrus is tired of warfare«, Sargon replies, »and he was strongly opposed to the introduction of a mercenary army by Marius.«

»He will certainly listen to someone like you. A man who stands for our guilty conscience. A man known for profound philosophical reflections, especially when it comes to people, to all people! Do I need to be more clear?« He waits briefly, but only to highlight the absence of a reply. »He also has such a streak«, he continues. »After the victorious campaign against the Thracians, there were serious assaults and ill-treatment of the prisoners, which he vigorously prevented.«

»Why, by Zeus, you want him in command then?«, asks Sargon.

»Because we need a man with experience who won't let the accomplishment of this task go to his head. Someone who willingly moves back to his civilian life without much fuss.«

»If that's it«, Sargon replies, »I have heard all for today.« He rises, glances briefly at Sertorius to assure him that he cannot be held this time, and leaves the Curia without a greeting.

At the exit of the Curia, he pauses for a moment, looking indecisively over the stone-tiled square, *what is this going to be?*

»Ave, Sargon«, he suddenly hears a voice out of the dark, makes him instantly remembering his encounter with Thrajan of Aqiun, but the voice is all too familiar. He keeps his eyes straight ahead, so as not to give this oaf the satisfaction he hopes for, by his sudden appearance out of darkness. From the periphery of his perspective he recognizes Antonius Dolobella, striding gravely toward him.

»Forgive my sudden appearance. I don't intend to impose a long conversation on you, - though...«

»Yes«, Sargon answers briefly, before Dolobella falls into a stammer, thus keeping him in the belief of a meaningful encounter. With a short gesture he motions for him to accompany, also to get the conversation over with quickly.

»Sertorius' idea of finding the Thracian's wife and starting a turnaround has failed. What else can we do?«

»I don't know«, Sargon replies. »But I don't think the Thracian would negotiate anything with us. I'm sure he hates us more than we'll ever hate him.«

»Some believe he is descended from Thracian princely houses.«

»Of course some believe it, it's spread with great zeal. It doesn't please the rich patrician families, it doesn't please most Romans, that our legionnaires, victorious in all the world, cutted down by a runaway slave.«

»That's precisely why I don't believe it's just a rumour.«

»So?«, asks Sargon in what appears to be an interested tone, »you've heard something, about a ransom, offered from Thrace?« Sargon senses Dolobella's desperate search for an answer, knowing it will not come, *clumsy, he will evade, without shame.* Suddenly he remembers the conversation with Annaeus when it was still about containing the uprising on Vesuvius. *Curse on the state of mind*, he thinks. *The Thracian noble or not, that's what they worry about. They will drag us all down the abyss, we deserve it.*

»You really believe he's just a slave, a gladiator?«, asks Dolobella with a put-on, suspicious undertone.

»I don't believe anything, I'm just saying what I know!«, replies Sargon, unfazed by undertone, with which Dolobella hoped to rid himself. »We sent both consuls against him and they failed shamefully. So, we start ennobling him. Now excuse me.«

»Sargon«, he calls, and again almost shouting: »Sargon, wait!«, Dolobella grabs his arm: »It takes two years to train a legionnaire, we need twice as many for our officers. And now tell me again that a slave, a tool, raises an army with which he crushes our legions!«

»Let it! You break my arm!«, and looks into Dolobella's wide open eyes. In a hushed voice, but slowly, as if each word has its own meaning, he answers him: »We drill them for two years so that even in battle they will follow an order rather than try to save their wounded comrade's life. You moron, what'd you think battle is like?«

Chapter 9.

Dives

»He has to fan me«, Decimus says indignantly, »it's hot in here! And tell him to stop crying, I can't see it.«
Abner moves his arm briefly. The boy flinches, then monotonously raises and lowers the fan again.

»I think his arm hurts«, says Abner.

»How dare you contradict me!«

»Decimus, listen to your teacher!«

Surprised, he turns his head and recognizes his father at the entrance to the hall. Marcus Glabrus walks slowly through the hall, stops next to the lad and examines him briefly. »How long have you been here?«

»Two hours.«

»You can go now. - Bring another lad«, he calls to the servants, »one who is less slight.« Then he glances at the papyrus scrolls and drawings on the blackboard. »Go on with him now, Abner. I want to see how he's doing.«

Abner waits until the father has taken a seat a little apart and then continues. »Look, - the horizontal lines mark the positions of your legions. They are passing through a valley. Suddenly, on the crest of a hill, the enemy appears, what are you doing?«

»I'll send out my scouts and order the front legions to retreat, the two outermost legions march forward until they join up with the others to extend the battle line. I'll take back the rear legions. I won't deploy them until the scouts are back.

The remaining two I will let each march to the outside to intercept a possible attack from the side.«

»Good. Your scouts return, they tell you that the enemy's main forces are each on your left and right, advancing in haste marches.«

»If they suddenly appearing on the left and right, my scouts would have noticed before!«

»Perhaps you have been trapped, ambushed«, Abner replies, but without scorn, simple the same monotonous pronunciation of his previous sentences. That's why Glabrus had asked him to teach his son.

»Five of my legions are at the front«, continues Decimus.

»I let the rear ranks fall back in a pendulum-like motion to reinforce my sides.«

»I let the rear ranks fall back in a pendulum-like motion to strengten my sides.«

»The enemy, standing on a hill above you, would undoubtedly see this. Encouraged by the realization of how weak your flanks stand, he will fall upon them full of fury to break through, for then he can attack your legions in the rear as well.«

»But I still have three legions that I withdrew completely at the beginning.«

»That's why they'll be late. Never forget that the area where these movements take place can be several miles long and wide. Always think of the time that will pass before the legates have transmitted your orders. - So take the front legions all the way back when the enemy appears so suddenly. The front ones retreat and the rear ones move outward. In this way, your army stands in the shape of a crescent moon. This is the safest protection, even if the enemy has bypassed you.«

Decimus looks at the tablet, searching for clues to justify his actions again.

»I think we are good for today«, says Abner finally, turning to Glabrus. Decimus also turns to him, questioningly he looks in his fathers eyes.

»It was good, son. But don't always doubt what Abner teaches you. He was my companion in all the campaigns, remember that.«

»Yes father.«

»Good. Go now, Nikias is waiting outside with the horses.«

Glabrus waits until his son has left the hall to talk to Abner alone. »His treatment of slaves, the way he talks, orders them, his indifference to pain and suffering - as if he had never been in our house.«

»At his age«, Abner says, »most lads tend to be that cold, beliving it expresses their strengt.«

»Perhaps. But it is different with him.«

Their brief conversation is interrupted when a servant of the house appears with a papyrus scroll. »Ave, I care an invitation with me, addressed to you, Marcus Glabrus. Issued with the seal of Marcus Licinius Crassus.«

Glabrus's eyes narrow, »from Crassus?«, he asks.

»Yes.«

»He is here?«

»No. An legation of his house delivered the invitation.«

»It's fine. Thanks,leave us now.«

Glabrus opens the seal, skims the few lines and exchanges a glance with Abner. »Is there any inconvenience?«, the latter asks.

»An invitation, nothing more. Two days from now. What'd you think?«

»I think he knows they want you. For the new troops they are sending against the Thracian, or at least he believes so.«

»I wish I could send you«, Glabrus says angrily, »a gesture here, a whisper there«, and hands Abner the invitation, »among such political bustle I'm lost.«

Abner skims the few lines again. »He writes only of a meeting between you and him?«

»It doesn't matter. Crassus understands such wrangling. He has good connections, he knows how to bribe, he will know about many things. A hint here, a passing remark there...«

»Has my talking been of no use to you all these years?«, asks Abner, somewhat reproachfully.

»No. I'm Sorry. I forgot who I'm talking to«, he apologizes, rolls up the invitation again and puts it on the table. »Is there any news of any kind, from the Senate?«, he then asks.

»Not that much. There are still too many who don't want to see, or can't see. Therefore - how they think, talk - whoever listens to them might think it's still about a band of robbers going about plundering.«

»A hundred men«, says Glabrus, half to himself, »perhaps even a thousand, can be held together with the prospect of plunder. For ten thousand to follow, fight, a year, two years, it takes more than the promiss of plunder.«

»Sargon, maybe Annaeus too, are – probably the only ones who don't misjudge the situation. There is already a great loss of lands and wealth for many senators. With the losses, their fear grows, - power shifts that result from this or that decision regarding the rbellion. But let me tell you something that I heard yesterday from the women of our servants, happened in the house of Tiberius. Recently Annaeus wanted to sell some female slaves from his property to Tiberius. When they arrived at his house, they were dead. Tiberius was beside himself ...«

»Tiberius? You mean Annaeus?«

»No, I mean Tiberius. He screamed and yelled, running hysterically through his palace. The slaves have evaded his obedience, done something that shouldn't be. And worse still, as much as they are slaves, they express something with their suicide. They express distaste for Tiberius, for him as a person and as a man. About as much as an insult can be expressed by cynical politeness.«

»I don't know if I follow you, Abner. That Tiberius should run screaming through the palace I have often heard, and always they were reasons not understood even by those who spoke of them.«

»Perhaps so. But - let me speak plainly. I don't think they are blind to the danger, on the contrary. The Thracian, his victories, are - unreal, are, - the unknown. And that's why they fear him, even more than they feared Hannibal. For unlike him, the Thracian was a slave, a gladiator, and yet he leads his troops from victory to victory, against our legions. And besides the sheer fear of him, everyone is afraid to admit it, publicly or in the closed sessions of the Senate. For it would be tantamount to a renunciation. A renunciation of everything we believe in. And the hysterical demeanour of Tiberius makes it visible most clearly.«

Glabrus is accustomed to the manner of his friend speaking. Nevertheless, even he does not always find it easy to follow his words. But he has too often lent his ear to such intricate thinkers to throw their words to the wind. »It was good that Rome extended its influence of power to the Latins«, he says after a while, in order to say something at all and not to offend Abner.

»We should never have gone any further.«

»Yes«, Abner says in response. A ›yes‹ that reminds Glabrus of how much Abner spoke against it at that time.

»Shall we go to the porch?«, asks Glabrus whereupon Abner agrees, by mimicry that no one but Glabrus would notice as agreement.

»I can't promise you anything, not even some dates«, Glabrus says as they stand on the porch.

»I'll survive«, Abner says.

Standing silently next to each other, the two men pause as if they need to become familiar with a foreign environment.

»I liked this place, always have«, Glabrus says into the silence, »especially now, at twilight. I couldn't even say why.«

»It's the view of this boundless vastness«, Abner says.

»All immersed in melancholy, which sneaks in and entices and wants to capture us at all costs.«

Glabrus answers with an approving gesture and lets him know with a shorthand gesture that he could never have described it that way himself. Silently they pause again, gazing into the distance.

»Whenever you asked me onto this porch«, Abner breaks their silence, »there was something, - particular, something special on your mind.«

Patiently he waits, but since Glabrus does not answer, he gently tries to urge him again. »You have sympathy for the Thracian, don't you?«

»Perhaps«, Glabrus replies, opening his folded arms and leaning on the masonry in front of him. »They questioned a legionary who was present at the capture of Spartacus at that time. Sargon told me about it. There was a moment, an event, – the battle was already won, but our troops got into trouble again, so that the reserves had to intervene. They then pursued the fugitives, even though there was no order to do so. They found the Thracian in the enemy camp, in front of his tent. His wife dead, allegedly he killed her to protect her from desecration, the rest, - you know. I remember men, good men, who would have ended their lives in his place. At the latest when they find themselves in a gladiator school, which ultimately only poses the prospect of death. But he unleashes an unprecedented insurrection, in a country unknown to him. So, would you be very surprised if I answered your question with a ›yes‹?«

»No.«

»He wanted to cross the Alps with his people. What is he about to do now, what can he want now that it has failed? What is in store for us? For to leave the country, if he will, there remain only the Cilicians.«

»You don't think they'll do it? Take him out of the country, with their ships?«

»No. And if he should try to lay siege to a city to get ships, our legions would keep pushing him away. But even if he succeeds – the Adriatic is ruled by the Cilicians, they would not let him pass. If he goes to the west coast, he lacks the supply from the Cilicians.«

Glabrus straightens up again and places his hands at the side of his toga. »Some fear«, he then says, »that if the Thracians remain victorious, the insurrection may spread to the Latins, to the Samnites, Lucanians, Etruscans.«

»Possibly«, Abner replies, lapsing into brief reflection.

»Hannibal«, he then says, »came as an authorized commander of a state power, so did his troops. Yet he found few tribes willing to join him. The Thracian is a commander of slaves.«

»The core of his army is made up of gladiators, from Ravenna, Capua, Pompeii?«

»It doesn't matter«, Abner replies, with his usual cool, calculating manner that always brings something choppy to his pronunciation as well.

»Among the slaves who run to him there will certainly be Latins, but slaves after all. In the perception of a free Latiner, they are below him. Therefore, that the ancient tribes rise, to join a slave army, - no.«

Glabrus stares at the trees' foliage, which hints at its true structure whenever it emerges undulating from the semi-darkness. »So he stands alone«, he resumes the conversation.

»Even more so if you consider the fallen Gaul Crixus, as a kind of, - ally. You see no way out for him?«

»You wish I had one?«, says Abner in response, but more as a hint than as a question, and goes on immediately: »If you asked the question not to me, but to the Senate, you'll find yourself at court, the very next day.«

»I suppose so. That's why I'm asking you.«

»The Gaul may have been more than an ally. In the gain of a friend there is solace for painful loss. If this too is suddenly wrest away, prudence can finally succumb to vengeance.«

Abner pauses, whether his thoughts on the sensitivities of a friendship. Here, on this porch, like an equation to the friendship between him and Glabrus. Embarrassed, he seeks distance from his words, shooing away one of the beetling insects that run up the stone column beside him with the awkward movements of someone who is kown as more than just sophisticated somehow.

»No, I don't see a way out«, and falls back into a moment's thought again. »But it doesn't make the insurrection any less dangerous. Whoever fights only for his freedom, says 'no' so decisively to being slaves and gladiators, has little to lose and will take up the sword all the more bitterly.« Abner pauses, as he finds himself with sensitivities. »Is it possible that he will march against Rome itself?«

»Abner, that seems even more hopeless to me than the ancient Latin tribes might join him.«

»Have we not reason to suppose that the Thracian, is equally aware of all the desperateness? - That Rome also lies on the west coast would balance itself out, since our troops would then be tied up. The city would be defenceless if they tried to bypass him, to get between him and the Cilicians. But even if – even if I'm wrong, completely beyond the realm of possibility, – a demon in hopelessness no longer asks for meaning and usefulness. He seeks where he can to take everything with him, to death. - What would you do?«

Glabrus runs his hand over his forehead, noticing how this gesture now betrays his embarrassment, and directs his gaze again into the distance. »I would lay siege to Rome, with catapults and wall-breakers. - No, he doesn't have those. I would try to come to terms with the Cilicians. No, - no way to win them, not for him, not on our soil. I would, - my friend«, and turns his gaze to Abner, »I don't know.«

Even if the conversation was not heated, he wants to let Abner know how much he cares to know him at his side. Unexpectedly, this recalls Abner's decriptions of another friendship. The two men look at each other, for a brief moment, and suddenly feel again the menace of this rebellion, which remained hidden during their conversation. But both avoid the attempt to put it into words.

Glabrus glances at the clepsydra. »It's late. You have to leave?«

»Yes I must, my friend«, Abner replies.

»Well, let's go then. The horses are on the other side today.« Abner holds him back. »You did not ask me if I would advise you to go into the field against this enemy, as you usually do?«

Glabrus stops. »No, I didn't«

Abner hesitates, regrets suddenly of having reminded him of that question. »No«, he then says.

»Maybe you're right« Glabrus says, looking down as if searching for fleeting thoughts to add, but finally just says,

»Let's go.«

Abner adjusts himself on his horse when Glabrus asks him about Tiberius again: »The slave woman, who were sold to Tiberius, – how did they kill themselves?«

»When they heard that they are about to be sold to Tiberius, they hanged themselves, on their way there, with their chest bands.«

»I'm surprised you want to see me«, says Glabrus, says Glabrus, as it were by way of greeting, deliberately ignoring formalities, examining Crassus, while a slave pours him wine. He seems more corpulent to him, his short bull neck, but doesn't seem rounded or obese at all. His eyes, tense as ever, give him something repulsive, which contradicts his well-known hospitality.

»Sit down, have a seat«, Crassus nevertheless asks him with his usual courtesy, without injecting any sort of cynicism into his pronunciation. »Sargon and some of his white-haired henchmens will come to you tomorrow to place you in command of new troops. I want you to decline their offer.«

»I've already said ›no‹ once. I can't send them away again.«

»Oh yes you can! And so will you!«

»Is that a threat?«, Glabrus replies matter-of-factly.

»All I want is for you to keep refusing. I'm sure your family will appreciate it.«

»Sargon is a friend of our family, so if he comes tomorrow ...«

»Will you refuse«, Crassus interrupts him as he reaches for his mug. »There are not a few to whom your behaviour and talk is a stone in the shoe. Your talk of dealing with slaves, their husbandry conditions, care and the like«, Crassus adds as he notices Glabrus' provocative, questioning look. »Of course, they are all far too busy to take this on. But sometimes a single word is all it takes.«

»You would do that? For what? To enter the city even once like Pompey under trombones with a victorious army?«

»By Zeus, so it is!«, hisses Crassus in a rage. »When Sulla fought Marius, he was almost defeated. He owed the victory to the right wing, which I led, yet nothing left of that glory for me. Today everyone is afraid of this Spartacus. Have you heard, the Thracian defeats two consuls at once, he is the son of a Thracian count, he deserved to be born a Roman!« Then he presses out between his lips, »And it will be me who destroys his army. I will restore Roman honour in arms.«

»Just tell them the truth that everyone knows: that Marius' decisions to form a standing army displeased you.«

»There is no way they will accept that.«

»Then add family matters. Was not a daughter recently born to you? Refuse their requests, repeat your reasons, and after a while they will leave. Annoyed, no doubt, but it won't be your harm.«

Glabrus gives him no further answer. Silently, without looking at each other, the two men face each other. With cold eyes, Glabrus straightens his toga and declares this way the conversation to be over. He takes a step aside to pass Crassus when he speaks up once more. »When they come to you tomorrow, do as I have asked you this day. You have nothing to fear. Even if someone should act against you, – I have arranged for the necessary. A request to investigate your case would be denied, due to other pressing circumstances.«

»Of course. That too can be bought.«

*

Aristotle

Sargon reluctantly takes on the punishing sea voyage, but after Glabrus could not be won over, much to the displeasure of Sertorius, he proposed Crassus himself. And also said that it's needed to seek him out, to at least hint, that they were willing to give him command of the troops, and to see, to hear how he would respond. Above all, but he kept this to himself, he did not want to wait until Crassus himself would appear in Rome, after he heard from Glabrus how strong he urged, to lead troops against the Thracian. For he would demand, he would set conditions. *There is still time*, he thinks. *A month, maybe two, then Crassus himself will come. The fear of the Thracian and his 'hordes', will drive nobility and senate into his arms, all the more because it's unspoken. All the more, since the Thracian will probably remain victorious. Hardly to assume that this will change.*

Finally arrived in Sicily, a sedan chair is waiting to take him to the villa of the richest citizen of Rome, Marcus Licinius Crassus, who is therefore also called ›Dives‹.

Sargon takes a look at the chair and the surrounding countryside. No one to be seen except the bearers. The 'Dives' obviously avoids receiving him personally, in order to put this visitation as low as possible and thus to dispel any rumour, any interpretation, any assumption that could point to his hopes. Sargon expected something similar, but not so clearly. He wrestles with himself, thinks of turning back again, of abandoning the whole project. *Who am I helping? Return to*

Rom? No! Crassus would come himself, offer himself, ingratiate himself, with the nobility, with the Senate. No, it must be today.

Would he accept the supreme command? Yes, of course! What would he ask for? How does he see this insurrection? It has to be today, to lure him, to make him believe in a few months it might be too late. The interrogation of the legionary in the Curia comes back to his mind, to find the Thracian's wife. *He killed her. War and destruction we bring over the world, the Thracian now brings it back. Who am I helping? Maybe I should help him? Cato hoped the Thracian over the Alps, maybe he is right after all? Maybe the Thracian will succeed in leaving the country. Fair it would be, would be against the aristotelian school of thought. Crassus is not averse to philosophy. No, he is not, even fond of it. Perhaps there will be an opportunity to help him to leave the country. More you can not do and more is not possible for anyone.*

He suddenly feels the waiting, questioning looks of the bearers. Even if they would never dare to question him, he wants to create distance between them and his moment of reflection. Awkwardly he bends his corpulent figure and reaches for a shell, as if he had been looking for it all along. *May it look funny*, he thinks, *rather than the other way*. Then he walks the few steps from the shore to the sedan chair and lets himself be helped in. *He should have sent horses, That way, it'll take another hour*, yet keeps his anger for himself, *everything but that.*

When he is only a few steps away from the entrance gate, he notices Crassus on one of his terraces, from where he has a good view of the way to his estate. The 'Dives' looks down at him from above, his right hand raised in greeting, which Sargon half-heartedly returns.

The bearers stop, a slave helps him out of the chair and leads him up the steps. At last Crassus appears to receive his guest in person.

»Be welcome in my house, Sargon. Forgive me for not receiving you while you were still in port. In these difficult days, some things must remain undone.«

Sargon returns the greeting, but does not say a word about the unworthy appearance. *He may think his hour has come*. Both walk silently side by side, slaves open a two-part door, and they enter a large, bright room. In the centre a table, surrounded by wooden, richly decorated chairs. Behind, somewhat separated, other conveniences, to which Crassus invites his guest to sit down, with gallant pronunciation reserved for such moments. A slave fills two golden cups with wine and departs.

Sargon looks at the cascades descending from the magnificent vaults and filling a basin from which an artificial stream leads outside. The ›Dives‹ has lacked for nothing: He has had hills removed and refilled elsewhere, to create a landscape, entirely according to his ideas.

»How was the journey?«, asks Crassus.

»Tedious and far too long.«

»I see«, Crassus replies with a smile. »What concern moved you?«

»You already know«, Sargon replies, deliberately irritated to dispel any suspicion about his knowledge as to the true reasons for Glabrus' refusal, and continues speaking with a cynical undertone: »The threat posed by the army of slaves makes it necessary for all who love Rome and want to see it great to mobilize their forces to get quickly rid of this shameful situation for us.«

»You don't say. Who would have thought that I would ever hear such words from you.«

»Probably no one, that's why it's me speaking to you here today, to please you.«

Crassus, again with a thin smile on his face, looks at him.

»So«, he says then, repeating, slightly modified, his question: »What is the reason that you honour me?«

»Honour you? Don't be silly.«

»Not at all! Why it's you!? I believed Annaeus would come. Yet now it's you, in his stead?«

»That need not interest you! I have my reasons, we can't talk about it now-you know where it ends.«

»You think... «

»Let's say - I'm here to brief you«, Sargon interrupts him. »A first-hand situation report, for the richest citizen of Rome.«

»Speak!«, Crassus replies caustic, but immediately regrets showing himself sore. Not now, not here, should there be evidence again for all the talk that has grown up about his wealth: ›Crassus, a man with immeasurable riches, but no idea how to use them‹.

Half looking past Crassus, Sargon sits back, slowly, to linger in the moment and make his continuing speech his decision:

»Two weeks ago we placed another six legions under Cassius' command. It is not to be expected that he will subdue the Thracian. The whole country hovers in a lethargy that makes, - all more worse, more difficult, more dangerous. The insurgents maintain good relations with the Cilician pirates.

They supply them with ore, weapons, all kinds of war equipment. And our legions«, Sargon continues hesitantly, »the ones we've sent out so far have been worn down.«

»So you're asking me to wage war against this rabble. That's what you're here for? Or?«

Sargon hesitates, since Crassus speaks of mobs, and does not otherwise announce anything about desires for glory, fame equal to a Pompey. »We will raise new legions. Not three or four, but an army. Then we will assign a general, one who knows how to lead such a mighty force.«

Crassus has risen and glances at him briefly, out of the corner of his eye. Sargon's hands folded over his doublet, his eyes two sickles, his words so self-evident, not a hint, not a finger pointing to other possible candidates beside him. He didn't expect it to be so obvious. He turns his back to the senator, lets his right hand slide slowly over the marble column and raises it to shoulder height, as if he has to think about something important.

»This leader, what's his name?«, he asks in slow words, groping his way, as if in a dark night, on unknown territory.

»Spartacus«, replies Sargon.

»Spartacus«, Crassus repeats.

»When he raided the South at the beginning of the rebellion and the slaves ran to him, he sent for a scribe and told him to write down exactly what work all the - had done so far. Then he sent a large part of them back, it is said, especially to the armorers. And because he lacked ore, he had the iron gates of the slave quarters melted down.«

»What's so surprising about it?«

»Aren't you surprised!?«, replied Crassus, upset.

»No. Why should I? He is the son of a Thracian prince, isn't he!«, leaving no doubt about the sarcasm of his reply.

»You seem to doubt this?«, asks Crassus in a demanding tone.

»Is that of interest?«, replies Sargon, equally demanding, knowing he hits a sensitive point. »You know what I think of it«, he then continues to speak in order to relax the situation,

»yet I didn't come here to settle deep philosophical questions about the 'Why' and 'Wherefore' a man is a slave or a master.«

Crassus presses his lips together, opens them again with an audible breath, as is often seen with him, on the verge of an angry outburst, but this time he has himself under control.

»You hide, as you often do, behind the arrogance of the wise mind«, and waits then to see if Sargon wants to retort something, »be unconcerned, no need to settle deep philosophical questions, because I have the answer here.«

He reaches into the papyrus holder and pulls out one of the scrolls. »Read! It's an excerpt of a letter from Aristotle, a wise mind that I know even you appreciate«, and hands him the papyrus scroll, yet pulls it back then. »It will be better if I read it to you!«, unrolls it and reads to him:

> » ›Those who are as different
> as the soul from the body
> or man from beast are slaves by nature.
> For them it is better to be ruled in accordance ,
> to be in that kind of servitude.‹

Well then. Those whose task is to use their physical strength and for whom this is the highest achievement!« he summarizes what he has read and directs his gaze to the seated Sargon, who does not return it, but answers him, with an inflexion as if he had to fight sudden melancholy: »I know these texts. I don't need any lessons.«

»I ask for a little patience please!«, Crassus passes over the objection.

›those are by nature slaves,

who may be owned by another,

which is why they are owned by another,

and who participates in reason only insofar,

as he hears it in others,

without possessing it himself.

The slave, is only little different

from the domestic animals.

Both do not hear the voice of reason,

but are governed and guided exclusively

by emotional impressions and

sensual sensations. ‹ «

»And? What does he write about domestic animals?«, asks Sargon, burying all hopes of finding an ally in Crassus, at least on these issues.

»What!?«, asks Crassus, deliberately confused, as if he had not heard correctly.

»If the slave is what Aristotle said it is, then there is no need for these fine, conclusive considerations. But he thought it necessary. So he will have written also about pets, to what extent they differ from us, - I suppose.«

»He does! In these very lines, which I just left you! Both are little different from each other, he writes! Not reason guides them, but emotional impressions!«

»So they are animals, even pets, without any doubt! Then what's the point of such a edifice of ideas?«

Crassus doesn't answer, just looks at him, rolling up the papyrus again demonstratively.

»Why did he ever write this?«, continues Sargon »Why did he take time to think about it, to write it down? - Did he want to ease his conscience because he couldn't get past the fact that these pets ultimately have two legs, two eyes, a mouth to speak, outwardly no different from us? Was the zeitgeist of his time charged with doubts from which one wanted to feel free again? And he gave the zeitgeist what it craved? Why? To ease our consciences? Have you ever thought about it?«

»No never! For I don't doubt!«

With an angry, dismissive wave of his hand, Sargon returns to the topic at hand. »How is it that you study these scriptures so closely?«

»The situation is serious, as you said yourself. People lose faith in Rome. In such times it is important to remind the people of glorious days and of people with whose names they associate the greatness but also the goodness of Rome.«

»What you wanna do? Passing out this letter among the people?«

»A good idea, but I'm afraid most Romans, especially those who hold you in high esteem, wouldn't be able to read it. You came to me to offer me command of the troops!? Even if you haven't actually said it yet, we both know it is! I won't take it, unless it's more than slave-hunting!«

»Shall Rome, the Senate itself, knight them?«

»Spare me your sarcasm«, Crassus replies sharply.

»They are slaves«, Sargon says firmly, »we can call them gladiators from now on. What's the use?«

»Nothing! But the situation in which Rome finds itself is called war. Say it, name the danger. Ultimately, it's not just about defeating this wretched enemy. It's about who we are, what we are. We are the civilization! We are people of education, have a sense of culture and arts. A sense for goodness and beauty in this world. You understand!? Thats what WE are and not the slaves!«

»They will be very surprised in the Senate, wondering, when I tell them that it is you, who are now calling for this insurrection to be called war.«

Unmoved, Crassus lets this remark drip off himself. Emphatically slowly, he puts the wine cup back on the table.

Sargon rises. »The Senate will think about it.«

»Good«, Crassus says in response, waiting until the old man is only a few steps away from the exit of the house. »Sargon«, he then calls after him, the way one calls after an adolescent to give him some more good advice along the way. »He killed his wife. What a barbaric, wooden nature, don't you think?«

»No«, is Sargon's immediate reply, »an act of love. Devoted, intimate love. - They lived somewhere in the Thracian hills, took their goats to pasture in the morning, picked berries, and went to bed together at night.«

»Goats and berries«, Crassus repeats, as for a noting.

»Yes Crassus, goats and berries. Suddenly, an enemy army approaches and crushes everything. Maybe she even asked him to. Begged to help her out of life. Is that possible, Crassus? Can you imagine that?« Out of the corner of his eye, Sargon sees his counterpart tilt his head with a puzzled, questioning expression on his face. For a moment there are words on his tongue that demand to be uttered, but with a jerk-like movement he turns away. These poor spirits. Waving briefly his hand, to say goodbye only fleetingly, he leaves the house.

Chapter 10.

War Machinery

The sun is low as the Senate gathers. Drusus, the young officer to whom Praetor Varinius owes his survival, has arrived in Rome late this afternoon. Two months ago, the Senate sent him north, to the area around Placentia. He was ordered to watch over the happenings there, and, if necessary, return to Rome immediately, reliable sources are needed. Drusus' report of the combat zone in the north ran through the city at a pace that only really threatening news reaches.

Frantically the assembly is convened and within a short time the temple of Concordia is filled with prefects, senators and nobles. Tensely they listen to Drusus' words: »He has already turned his troops, in the next few days they will reach Ravenna. the Cilicians are meant to expect them there, probably.« Gasping, at the complete silence that has spread, he stays in the middle of the hall, looking into the faces around him.

»Did you see it yourself or were you just told about it?«

»I saw it myself. There were rumours that the Thracian was about to die. Was said, explained as the reason that they didn't move on for so long.«

But we couldn't find out anything specific about it.« Drusus' tension subsides, hearing murmurs and whispers now, seeing Heads leaning to the side. Lutatius rises, a middle-aged senator who presides today. »It is a disgrace to see Rome in such great danger. Threatened by an army of slaves, led by a slave descended from a barbarian people.«

»We know it's a disgrace«, an old man rises. »But what to do about it?« He continues, with a voice trembling with anger:

»Thousands of young men, Romans, lie on the battlefield, including my son. Because you don't want to see...«, he gasps for air as anger takes his breath away, »...don't see the danger...« His fists clench, his arms twitch, whirling through the air as if to catch there the words he needs. »You call the Thracian a barbarian, still...«, searching for support, he reaches for the man next to him. He wants to continue, but suffocated by the fiery atmosphere in the hall.

»Cassius was given command against his will«, echoes through the hall, »we are indebted to him.«

The hall trembles, but in a different way than usual, not as in political disputes. Whipped up by hysteria are their spirits. Drusus feels a tremor spreading through him, a tremor that overcomes him in excited situations and against which he is powerless.

»What should we thank him for, or the others? For their bungling, with which they sent two armies to their deaths?«, it shouts from the other side. The tumult intensifies, desolate insults from all sides, hardly possible to make oneself understandable.

Sargon rises. Not expecting anyone to take notice, he slowly descends the steps to the altar and stands next to Drusus.

»Is Spartacus«, with that name and his booming bass, makes the hall stop the clamour and turn to him. »Is Spartacus that strong by now? Are we already so afraid of him that the Senate, the power centre of the Roman state, is falling apart?

Men who are supposed to be paragons of virtue are acting like market standholders!«

»I am leading the assembly today«, Lutatius interrupts him.

»We have extraordinary circumstances that require extraordinary action«, Sargon replies without looking at him.

»Spare us your admonitions«, Cornelius resounds through the hall, his neck stretched forward and his voice shrieking as always. »What's your proposal? You yourself? Leading our legions?«

Artificial laughter from his patrons. It was always artificial, but today it sounds more tortured than ever and seeps sickly.

Drusus looks slightly to the side, to see if Sargon will answer Corneluis. But the latter, with a turn of his body, accentuated facial expressions and gesticulation, lets it be known that he will not pay any attention to the shouter. He waits until the hall has calmed down again and then continues speaking, with clear, decisive pronunciation: »Remus«, Sargon glances briefly at the old man, »a father lost his son, like many others. Would anyone like to weigh which lost son was worth more!?«, and letting his gaze wander through the silent hall. »Hm!? How many sons will we send this time, to their deaths? Five Legions? Ten? Cassius was send against his will, we just heard. Against his will, because the Thracian is 'only' a Babar, leader of a horde of slaves. Clodius believed the barbarians were trapped, back then on Vesuvius. Two years ago! After that we sent Varinius, who wouldn't even have survived without the help of his officer, which you see here before you. Then Cossinius and Furius, with two armies each. Then Gellius and Lentulus, our two consuls, - yet they too achieved nothing. Of their legions only the name remained.«

Lutatius, who was supposed to be leading the hearing, interrupts him: »I have an inkling of what you are driving at!«, and rises, slowly. »Impossible!«

Again unrest in the hall, and the unspoken, the uncertainty that lies in Lutatius' words, causes the hall to boil again. The few who have understood wave their arms in pleading for silence.. »We can't«, Sargon wants to continue, but waits until the last ones rest. »We cannot ennoble the rebellion, cannot exalt the Thracian, or his horde of slaves. We can't even call them a gladiator army. Even that would be interpreted as weakness. But we can proclaim one, ONE Consul, with full powers, and at least ten legions under his command!«

Again a roar rises: »That would be fifty thousand men... with full powers... what's that meant to be!? ...dictatorship!?... The proclaim of dictatorship«

Sargon raises his arm asking for silence: »These are serious questions, but before the Senate fulfills its duty to settle them, I would like to ask our young officer to leave the assembly for the time being. Drusus, we thank you. It was very prudent of you to inform us. Go now, please. May the gods be with you.«

*

Marcus Licinius Crassus is neither a senator nor a prefect. Still, no one would have denied him access to the Comitium today. But it would be detrimental to his intentions, for not he himself, wants to propose to the Senate to proclaim him Consul. No, they should come to him, ask him. The threat of the slave army is has grown much greater. Nevertheless, he believes the time has not yet come to offer himself as Rome's saviour. The Thracian, descendant of princely houses, a rumour, that Crassus had stirred up, this would have been a bridge to ask for the supreme command himself, publicly, but it had evaporated. *Who else is there but me? What if Glabrus recants his refusal?* For hours, the same questions torment him. *Who can be entrusted with an army, who else is there who has stood his ground in the field? They will come to me. I need someone to point a finger, someone to remind them who led the right wing under Sulla.* The news about the advance of the slave army has also reached him. But he does not want to rely on Sargon alone. So he orders his servants to wait near the Comitium to ask Annaeus to meet him.

*

»So. You want me to remind them that there is still a Marcus Crassus?«, asks Annaeus, sitting down without Crassus having offered him a seat to keep him believing that although he has complied with his request for this conversation, he is only smiling at his it.

»What's so dislike about it?«

»Who cares if I dislike it?«, retorts Annaeus. »If I mention your name tomorrow, why do you think they should go for it?«

»You are not only to mention my name, you are to remind them WHO led the right wing under Sulla at that time. It was me!«

»There are others besides you with war experience.«

»Well, who are you thinking of? Glabrus?« Crassus feels that he has the old fox in his pincers, no rhetoric, no amount of diplomatic skill will help him, and continues, »he was victorious in Thrace, he was. With a threefold superiority. I'll save myself from doing the math for you. And - you humiliated

him deeply at the time, you would make yourselves ridiculous in front of everyone if you now proclaimed him Consul.«

»Need I remind you how you got your wealth? There are even rumours that you yourself set fire to houses.« Crassus wants to interrupt him, but Annaeus continues to speak as if he had a student in front of him, knowing that it is precisely this disparagement that hits the ›Dives‹ the most.

Just may he be offended, Annaeus thinks, watching his up and down across the room. The Senate is not an institution to give orders to, even with over seven thousand talents. »The richest citizen in Rome and now we're giving him an army?«

Crassus bites his lips, almost succumbing to the old man, by saying things, stirred by a flaring anger, that would not only ruin this conversation, but all previous efforts. »I am probably not only the richest citizen of Rome«, he replies, feigning composure, »what could possibly displease the Senate? It should be a further reason, to persuade him to give me command of the legions.« He pauses, but since Annaeus does not answer, he continues, with a demanding tone: »Make them sure about the danger Rome is in. An army of slaves, sixty thousand, they will wreck Rome, wipe out its population, till nothing left. They will plunder, burn our lands, and there is no other way than to proclaim a Consul who has proven himself in the field.« Energetically, with flashing irascibility, he goes on:

»Annaeus, I beseech you, if you name me, many veterans who fought with me in Sulla's army will join us. With these legions we will strike down the Thracian, this spring.«

»What makes you think he will march against Rome?«

»What is left for him? His escape across the Alps has failed. He's moving south to resupply. And then? Cross over to Sicily? He would be even more of a prisoner there than here. North again? No! Leave the country by ship? But the Cilicians rule the Adriatic. They will neither help him, nor will they let him through, in case he manages to procure ships himself. Shall I go on talking?«

»No«, Annaeus replies, but appears unimpressed. He impassively averts his gaze from him before he starts to speak further: »I see that you are willingly«, he finally says. »What do you see, looking at this riot? Slaves? Just slaves?«

»If I didn't know it was you, I would assume Sargon...«

»What if he's right!?«, Annaeus cuts him off, but skilfully, placed, not admonishing. »I don't share his attitude any more than you do. But that's not the poin heret, it's to end this shameful war, to defeat this wretched enemy. Weren't these your words when Sargon was with you? That's why I'm asking you, what do you see!?«

»When he was with me, I made it clear to him that I would always refuse the command as long as you talk about slave hunting instead of war!«

»It's not enough for us to ennoble this 'slave hunt' for you. What about yourself? What danger do you see?«

»I see, – savage barbarians!«

»That's it!?' That's why you long for it?! That's why you seek so despertly for a battle with him? Hoping for glory, like a Pompey!?«

»In public, these will always be my words. If we are here, in dialogue, let me tell you this. Sargon asked questions, simple questions, about the writings of Aristotle. There are not a few wise minds of another school of thought who would unhesitatingly claim that Aristotle is one of the pillars on which slavery rests. To own slaves, to let them work, torture them, take them to bed, all self-evident. Because serving others is best for them, that's all they're good for. So or similarly he wrote it down.«

»I know very well that you can be as enthusiastic about philosophizing as Sargon. I'm not. Therefore, a simple objection. Let me walk the streets tomorrow and ask for a pillar on which slavery is based on, do you think I'll find someone who says he has Aristotle's permission or some kind of nonsense?«

»No! But tomorrow go through the streets and ask why they follow this or that omen? Ask about obscure religions they are in bondage to, oblations they offering their gods. You will also find no one who could answer this. That there are slaves in this world is an evolved belief. Just like the belief in all the insanity that religions spread. With every defeat our troops, the faith, the pillar, whatever, becomes weaker, becomes unstable. That's why, - that Thracian out there, it's not just any insurgency« Crassus slowly walks to the other end of the table and then turns back to Annaeus to read his countenance with some distance, for he had no intention of winning him over with philosophy and now sees himself in turn in distress.

Also, because it suddenly seems to him that Annaeus lured him there. But apart from a questioning look, nothing is to be taken from his features.

»Sounds like even the Dives has doubts, - about our slave world?«

»No! I have no doubts about it! Neither that there are slaves, as described in the scriptures, nor that they are here to master them. Can you say the same of Glabrus!? Ask our nobles, our senators! Barbarians they will say, nothing else.«

Annaeus feels reminded of the conversation with Sargon, almost two years ago, when it came to similar questions.

»What do we know about the Thracian?«, asks Crassus, since Annaeus remains in silence.

»Nothing, except...«

»That he killed his wife!?«, adds Crassus demanding.

»To get rid of ballast!?«, Annaeus replies just as demanding, but immediately regrets this impulsive answer, for he sees in Crassus' face that it was his intention to provoke him to this reaction. »Perhaps we know something more«, he continues, but very slowly, very measuredly, in order to gather his thoughts, for he remembers how Sargon also spoke of it when they last met. And he admitted to himself what he never thought possible, but he wants to prevent this from becoming a subject now. Crassus is meant to win this war, it doesn't matter how he conceives this thracian-wife-event. »Perhaps a little more«, he ties in, repeating his pre-words, »and that's something again that speaks for Glabrus, he said: ›A hundred men can be held together with plunder,' but tens of thousands?‹ Sounds like a man who sees the danger more clearly, than you.«

»Ten thousand plunder less?«

»No! - Yet you overlook - Teutons and Gauls under Hannibal, were mercenaries, fighting for glory, hoping for spoils of war. The men who follow the Thracian, fight because something was taken from them, wherefore they hate us from the bottom of their souls. They will not march against Rome. They will fight to get out of this damned country, because here they will find only death anyway, which they therefore no longer fear«, the last word is hardly out of his mouth when Crassus gives free rein to his irascibility. »Again, I would assume that Sargon is speaking to me and not a senator known for orgies and drinking sprees where every guest is lavishly provided with beautiful virgin slave girls!«

»Then take a phrase from Sertorius: ›My thoughts are directed solely to the suppression of the insurrection‹, said thus or similarly in the Comitium, when it was still a question of finding the wife of the Thracian. ›As soon as this rebellion collapses, my thoughts will find itself again in old, familiar ways.‹«

»Good! Now let me teach you. I know about the victory over the Gallic Germanic bunch, which wasn't one. Spare me your objections, I know it is known to you as well as to me. And more. They almost overran Gellius because he didn't want to wait, because he wanted the victory for himself alone. Usual competition between two consuls. Lentulus came to the rescue, though, thank the gods.«

»You believe in them!?«, Annaeus head flies forward.

»You don't!?«

Annaeus replies with a thin smile, as is often seen on Crassus' face, without trying to hide the imitation.

»It's not just a matter of«, Crassus becomes caustic, »defeating this wretched enemy!«, looking him firmly in the eye, making clear that his brief theatrical imitation does not impress him. »From what I hear, including from you, it seems downright important to repeat this whenever necessary. Take Glabrus, if you believe a soft hearted slave friend, a man tired of warfare, will fight down this rebellion. - How may you choose him? As Consul? Without a second beside him?«

»We can't appoint you either, without a second aside you! Unless you have something to offer!«

*

Marcus Licinius Crassus is proclaimed Consul the following day to sustained applause. Clad in a snow-white toga, he appears between the pillars of the rostrum, to enjoy the unexpected cheers of the masses. *This is my hour, this is truly a fateful day.* Exalted, he raises his arm, and the crowd shouts his name enthusiastically.

Standing on the steps of Basilica Julia, Sargon looks down at the throng, Cato next to him. »So. Now Crassus«, says Cato in a colorless voice.

»You wonder why I laid the ground for him yesterday, at the Comitium? That's what it sounded like, right?«, he glances at his nephew and Cato agrees.

»If I hadn't said what I said no one would have. And in a month they would be pleading with Crassus, because the Thracian would probably be at our gates by then. In the end, old Remus prepared the ground; without him I could not have spoken as I did.«

»Wasn't it Glabrus that Sertorius wanted? And didn't Crassus summon Glabrus and urge him to refuse your offer?«

»It was never our offer. It was only Sertorius' whimsical idea. Annaeus didn't want him, in the end he was able to change Sertorius's mind. I didn't want him either, Glabrus is tired.

When he was victorious in Thrace, he arrived by surprise, with a threefold superiority. Ten years ago he would have been the right one and I would have agreed. Today it's ike sending him to his death. Crassus didn't need to know any of this. He got enough.«

»Sixty thousand legionnaires will march from Rome to fight an army of slaves.«

»Yes. Go on.«

»You know where I'm going with this.«

Sargon looks again at the masses below him. »Slaves, you know how we generally feel about them, about the barbarians beyond our realm. I remember a day, I saw a little boy playing, by a water, and it pleased me. Suddenly someone stepped out of the copse, hit the little one and dragged him away. I already had the needed words on my lips, to, - then I saw the slave ring.« He breaks off abruptly, in a manner typical of him. His gaze still on the masses below. Gestures and expression doesn't suggest any further words. »They are humans«, he unexpectedly, goes on. »Fathers and mothers, sons and daughters, whom we enslave. Crassus must win. Or the gods may help us then.«

*

The Senate grants Crassus the right to recruit six legions, and four more from the remnants of the defeated army, plus auxiliary troops. An army of this size had not existed since Sulla. One third of the immense costs for helmets, lances, swords, protective armor, in short, the entire equipment of the legionnaires, Crassus has to source himself. This is one of the conditions that the Senate imposes on Crassus for agreeing to

grant him the consulship for the duration of the war and not, as usual, for one year. The first preparations begin that very day.

Furthermore, an edict is issued to raise the finances for the construction of two hundred ships to stabilize the grain supplies. The effectiveness of the legions should not suffer from a lack of supplies. Declining combat morale will be countered with punitive transfers. The garrisons of the port cities will be strengthened in order to ward off raids by Cilician Pirates.

Rome pools its forces, mobilizes the entire war machine to finally put an end to the ignominious threat posed by the slave army.

Chapter 11.
Marcus L. Crassus

Sargon leaves the bedchamber and walks through the house, all quiet. These are the hours when the night ends, but the day still sleeps, when he feels free from all the hasty, quick decisions that the day will bring. Today there will be fewer, Miriam has been with them for a few weeks, she will take over some tasks as best as possible.

Alexandria, suddenly the name pushes itself into his thoughts. *The centre of our spiritual world has a female name, but women are denied a study. Miriam...she has disguised herself as a man.... took Cato into confidence...if only that goes well.*

He takes a few steps to gather himself so as not to sink into these thoughts. Cato will ride to the Roman camp today and he wants to give him some more on the way. Especially because of the new commander, Crassus, actually, only because of him. If only Cato wasn't such a ... well, he's a good kid, but a hothead. Crassus craves military success. He will demand iron discipline, no place for awkward customers.

Sargon stands in the centre of the portico, Miriam beside him while Cato dons his armor. »Crassus is quite open to new thoughts and reflections«, he says, »even fond of philosophy. But the Roman mother is sacred to him, you understand? Are you listening?«

»Yes«, Cato replies.

»He led the right wing under Sulla when they marched against Marius' army. Sulla owes him the victory, but he wa denied recognition. And here he is sensitive. So be careful with criticism of his decisions affecting any military strategy.«

»I'll be careful, but I don't think it'll come down to having anything to say about what he's up to. Unless he wishes it.«

»He will, as soon as he learns that I am your uncle.« Sargon says goodbye to his nephew rather coolly, which is not usually his way. But since Miriam is with them, *I leave the tearful goodbye to her.*

»I won't be here when you retun«, she says to Cato, »if you return.«

»I'm not about to fight there. I won't be anyelse than a legate. It's important to keep an eye on Crassus.«

»What does that have to do with the insurrection?«, Miriam asks, cautiously but demanding.

»Aristotle also wrote about slavery«, says Cato somewhat dryly.

»And!?«

Cato searches for words. He doesn't want to talk to her like a teacher talks to his student. »Just as he believed that female intelligence was inferior to that of male, so he believed that slaves are slaves by nature, that they are better off being mastered by others.«

»A revolt of slaves, is always a revolt against Aristotle, is that supposed to be it? And maybe I should be happy about it?«

»I don't know what it is yet. I don't think even Plato or his followers ever imagined that there could be such a insurrection. Crassus went out with an army, the likes of which was no greater against Hannibal. Something is happening here, and I want to see it. That's all I know, all I can say.«

Miriam looks at him with that look he can't avoid.

»The slave is deprived of everything worth living«, she says, »people who killed each other to escape their existence. And now, - hunger for life will drive them on, hunger for life. They certainly fear death less than returning to slavery. And that's exactly how they will fight you.«

»Yes«, Cato agrees, »that's what drives them.«

»Still, you are about to go?«, asks Miriam coolly, dryly, without looking at him.

»Don't talk to anyone about such thoughts; you won't find any spiritual relatives here in Rome.«

»Stop it«, she says with her feminine authoritative manner, »don't speak to me as if you were one of my advisors«, then she embraces and kisses him.

*

Cato does not hesitate and rides straight towards the group of horsemen who gather next to the consular tent. As he gets closer, he restrains his horse, exchanges a glance with the bodyguard, and then lets it trot slowly on, determined not to ask them to let him pass, but they block his way.

He does not acknowledge the guards with any greeting. Fixedly he stares in the direction of the Consul, whom he recognizes by his clothing and insignia: Marcus Licinius Crassus.

»I am not a courier of an enemy army, nor am I a legionary«, Cato says firmly.

Crassus waves his bodyguard briefly, whereupon they let him pass.

»You must forgive me«, he then says as Cato slowly approaches him. »But I couldn't resist giving you a little lesson in military order«, and takes a closer look at the arrival. »Well, what can I do for you, noble youth?«

»Ave, Consul. I am Cato Livius Sargon, a nephew of Senator Sargon; you sent for me.«

»Yes, right, - I had forgotten. Now that we meet on horseback, let's ride around the camp a bit.«

Cato lets his horse trot sideways beside Crassus' and looks at the bluish tents as they stand orderly, side by side at a well-measured distance.

»Well then. You are Cato, nephew of Sargon«, Crassus resumes the conversation. »A certain resemblance cannot be overseen.«

Cato politely accepts this statement with thanks, but otherwise restricts himself. The direction of the conversation seems him still too uncertain.

»I understand you have been in Alexandria for a long time, familiar with the writings of the philosophers, Aristotle, Plato and also the Sophists?«

Cato is initially surprised by the question, but Sargon's words come back to him. Only the mention of the sophists gives him cause for concern. But since there is no scorn at all, in his tone, though rather curiosity and interest, he finally answers.:

»I was there four years. And yes, -- I am familiar with their writings.«

Crassus casts a scrutinizing glance at him. »What drives such an educated man, as you are, into our camp? Be at ease, you are certanly welcome, but it seems to me that this is not the place for a philosopher.«

»I am here as one of your legates, at your service. Now and then it will be my duty to report to the Senate about the, - combat operations.«

»At Mars the Avenger«, says Crassus, visibly amused, »the campaign hasn't yet begun and the old fox has his eyes and ears on me already.« A little ironically, he adds, »You must know, Sargon and Me, - we share a special friendship.«

»I know.«

»Of course«, Crassus says in response with his typical thin smile on his face.

When they reach a spot from which they can overlook the entire camp, Crassus reins in his horse and halts it. »Look. Before you lies a Roman camp. The tents well arranged. An earthen wall the height of a small city wall surrounds them. Four gates, one at each point of the compass. This camp is the shelter and home of more than sixty thousand legionnaires. They embody our strength, our extended arm, in the north as well as in the south of the empire. But this time we have the enemy on Roman soil. And I ask you not as my legate but as a philosopher. How do they look on us? The Parthians, the Greeks, the Cilicians, seeing that we exhaust all our warlike possibilities to destroy an army of slaves?«

Cato looks aside for a moment, he didn't expect these kinds of questions from Crassus. »I can't answer that«, he says shortly.

»Are you afraid, Cato?«, Crassus asks, but doesn't wait for his answer. »Even a Consul needs more than an unsuitable opinion to have someone taken away. Above all, it would be an insult to my standing, my disposition, to denounce someone for reasons as such.«

»I'm not afraid, yet I'm not very familiar with military questions. I may say no more than, - if they are inferior to us in
  numbers, weapons, probably supplies, and they still defeat
us, it would certainly be very ignominious.«

»They have already beaten our troops, several times. So do
we have a dangerous enemy before us? Or just a wildly disor-
ganized bunch of slaves against whom we'll be leading legions
into the field in the next few days? Roman legions, victorious
all over the world?«

Cato hesitates. »I am surprised. I didn't expect such questions from a Consul named Marcus Crassus.«

An answer that puts a slight smirk on Crassus' face. »And?«,
he then asks.

Cato senses that he cannot avoid the question, but this is
the first day in the camp, Crassus will have to settle for a for-
mal answer: »Defeat means nothing but an insult to Roman
honour in arms.«

»Well, I follow your words, and say now, - therefore, all honours should be accorded to the commander who frees Rome
from this scourge. Would you disagree?«

Cato glances at the Consul again. »Why do you ask me? I am
only a legate. Whether I share these perceptions will be of little consequence.«

»Who else should I ask? My officers or my legatees? You are
Sargon's nephew, are here as my legate, still completely una-
ttached to the army. And you seem bold enough to answer
even if the answer displeases.«

Cato again hopes to be able to evade this question. Also the
denied glory comes back to his mind. However tolerant Crassus may pretend to be, - Cato urges himself to be cautious.

»The course of a war is often very mystical for a philosopher. As you said, the Thracian has defeated our troops
several times. To the commander who returns peace and security to Rome all military honours are due. Though he will not forget his sense of duty and therefore not use the victory for selfish demands.«

Crassus wants to respond, but his officers call for his attention. So he answers only briefly: »You are in the right place here, Cato Livius Sargon. We'll have many a conversation yet. Excuse me now.«

*

Crassus moves with his troops on the Via Flaminia north through Umbria. Then further east, near the city of Ancona. Sometime, in the next few days, his legions will meet the army of the insurgents. During the advance, he remains silent, seeks conversations only with those officers who already went to field with the armies of Cossinius, Gellius and Lentulus against the Thracian. In his mind he scans through their reports, lets the events of the past two years pass by and tries to classify the Thracian, to assess him. Him, who escaped with a handful of gladiators on Mount Vesuvius and begins a insurrection of unimagined proportions.

A slight discomfort, he suddenly believes to feel in himself, when he realizes that neither in the campaigns against Mithridates, nor against Marius, the leaders of the enemy troops had occupied him so intensely. The Senate had sent two armies to the Po Valley, but the Thracian remained victorious. Only through the perpetual battles, with the garrisons of the surrounding cities, was nevertheless achieved probably the most important goal for the Romans, not to let the slaves escape over the Alps. The scorn and derision of the Athenians would know no bounds. Above all, an army of insurgents, beyond the Alps, would be an incomparably greater threat.

After he has crossed the Apennines with his army and reached the coastline, he seeks the decision without hesitation. His insistence is rewarded, the first scouts return, carring news of the enemy's approach.

He gives his legions two hours' rest, then orders his troops to form up in battle formation and advances. Tense silence all around, the terrain flat, the sun at its zenith. After an hour, the horizon begins to move. The insurgent army, few miles away.

The thunderous ›bara‹ of the legionnaires rises, sixty-thousand are striking their shields with their swords.

Crassus reins in his horse, lets his eyes wander over the legions, when they are suddenly seized by a blood-curdling, demonic howl.

In an instant the distance is melted away and the army of the Thracian breaks upon the Romans with such force that the wings begin to sway, only thanks to the veterans standing in the centre can a breakup be prevented. Suddenly the insurgents retreat, dividing their lines, coarsening them. Crassus' legions, almost succumbed to the onslaught, still dazed, barely find time to realign with the centre. Even as they form up, a second wave rushes in, more violent than the first, and this time the flank breaks open. »Reserves forward«, Crassus hears the shouts of his officers. Completely rushed, the troops are brought up, but cannot stop the breakthrough.

Wild battle cries fill the air. Screams of pain and agony, of resentment and anger, rage like a storm that has suddenly risen over the landscape, taking everything with it.

Crassus has shouted his voice hoarse, riding along behind the lines as fast as the terrain allows. Over there, one of the legates appears. »Cavalry bound«, he shouts at the top of his lungs, yet barely audible, up the slope.

Crassus hesitates, gazes the centre again, with the veterans he already led under Sulla as they desperately try to hold off the attacks, then exchanges a glance with his commanders and gives the signal to retreat. A terrible howl floods the battle as the encircled legions realize they are given doomed.

Then the retreat, the retreat of the rest, – fails. Driven by panic many units lose contact with the main force and fall victim to the enemy cavalry.

Crassus moves back with his troops to the camp near Ancona, in Picenum, to make new recruitments, but also for fear of meeting the Thracian with his demoralized army. Between the mountain slopes of the Apennines, this would be the downfall.

The mood in the camp is more than just depressing, for the first battle against the Thracian joins in, in the succession of defeats. Now and then he rides through the camp, talks to his commanders, even to the ordinary legionary, but most of the day he spends in his tent. Once again he sees the force of the attack before him, the apparent retreat. *He did not let the whole army fight*, he suddenly believes, *only a part, and they retreated behind fresh lines*. How could I... Cato abruptly torn him from his thoughts when he enters through the tent entrance. »You sent for me?«

»Call the men together, war council. I have to brief them about our next steps.« Cato is halfway past the guards, who are already pulling back the entrance, when Crassus calls him

once more: »Cato!«, but then hesitates for a moment, as if he must weigh his thoughts once more. »You will ride to Rome, report to the Senate.« Questioningly, he looks at him. »I expect no embellishment, but let them know that this is the beginning. Marcus Crassus will bring down the slave army!«

Cato stands waiting at the tent exit, undecided whether to answer anything. »A strong, dangerous army turned against Rome. No one could expect us to be victorious immediately, even if they are only slaves.«

»You really believe that?«

»Yes.«

»Arguably. I am anxious to hear the report of your return, for you will not find approval in Rome with it.«

*

Parthian Rings

Four days after the defeat, Cato reaches the city of Asculum late in the evening. Here, far from Rome, the senators who have been entrusted with military duties await him.
When Cato enters the room, he immediately realizes that, in addition to the senators, representatives of the nobility of the surrounding lands have gathered.

Without further ado, he is asked to appear before the assembly and report to them on the progress of the fighting. All eyes are on him. A tension lies over the room that even breathing seems to be forbidden.

»We have casualties«, he then says into the silence. A low hum of whispers and gasps goes through the round.

»How many?«, asks Sertorius.

»It was a terrible onslaught, with many losing their lives. About 24.000 legionnaires fell.«

»Twenty-four thousand!«, echoes through the room several times. Cato sees bodies sagging, arms reaching up, hands covering desperate faces.

»And how many among the slaves?«, Sertorius continues to ask.

»We don't know exactly, there won't be more than a thousand.«

»And Crassus? He lives?«

»He is alive.«

»Speak up!«, Sertorius urges him.

»Crassus kept sending out scouts, who also brought news regularly. Some days more than three times. He was pressing for battle, to have the Thracian given as little time as possible to get an idea of our new troop strength. So he led our legions into battle at the first opportunity that presented itself. There had been no contact with the enemy until then. From what I heard ...«

»What's that mean!? What you heard? You were there!?«, someone from the nobility barks at him. Cato ignores the reproach and continues monotonously. »They rushed up. Suddenly there arose a terrifying, - roar, - scream, - as if from the throat of a demonic creature. It was as if heaven and earth were speaking with this voice. They were Parthian rings, as I was told later. - Finally the flank broke open - and - there was no longer any thought of an orderly retreat. In order not to perish completely, Crassus abandoned some of his Legiones.«

Breathing heavily, Sertorius exchanges horrified glances with the others.

»Where is his army now?«, he asks.

»He retired to Picenum, near Ancona.«

»Retreated?«, bursts out another of the nobility, hissing at Cato in voice overflowing with fear: 'I can hardly contain my anger. A massive Roman army is retreating, fearing the onslaught of an uncoordinated, savage band of slaves led by a barbarian! Is that so? Did I hear you correctly?«

Cato feels the speaker's gaze on him, though, facing the senators, he goes on: »May they be barbarians, slaves, whatever. This Thracian leads his troops with such prudence and they follow him as there is no death at all. He deceives, evades, embraces, and destroys.«

He lets his gaze wander through the hall. Although it is not a public hearing, five other influential senators are present in addition to the three Äerarii Militaris. Lowering their eyes, each seems lost in his own thinkings.

The nobility is finally compelled to leave the hall, they are not allowed to take part in the following deliberations.

After an interminable silence, Sertorius speaks to those remaining in a lethargically softened voice: »Crassus will make excavations, his ambition will drive him.«

»And if not?«, asks Sethos, from the group of five, slowly raising his head as if he has to wait till fears are fallen from his face.

»He will do it«, Sertorius continues, taking a few steps toward the wall as if it might provide an answer. »He has enough wealth to cover the costs«, With awkward movements of his arms, he backs away from the wall again. Wipes his hands then, over his face again and again, when he suddenly notices Cato.

»You're still here?«, he says to him with tortured kindness.

»Please leave us alone now.«

Cato says goodbye with a brief greeting and leaves the hall.

»Have the ships arrived?«, asks Sethos.

»Yes, they have«, replies Sertorius. »Don't get all your possessions on board, it would attract attention.«

Cato walks slowly to his horse. The animal comes towards him and gives a light snort. He strokes its nostrils, looking over the lifeless streets. *Who would have ever thought that the Senate could fall into lethargy because it feels threatened by an army of slaves.* Indecisive, he pauses for a while, finally setting off to seek out the senatorial night's lodging.

*

Sertorius watches the slave as he leads the horse away. Slowly he walks up the steps to the entrance of his house.

Suddenly a crashing sound behind him, startled he turns around.

»Forgivness, master. The horse became restless, it is not used to the surroundings.«

With half-open mouth, frozen in his movement, Sertorius looks at the slave. Then he regains his composure, but turns away without answering. With angular movements, he continues through the open swing doors. In the corridors leading to the thermae, his body slave Flacus comes to meet him and takes off his armor.

Sertorius looks at him insistently. Searching for features, for something suspicious. - are they tools?, he starts wondering while Flacus stands in front of him, his eyes downcast, and Sertorius continues to scrutinize him.

»Put the armor back on me«, he says gruffly, following every movement the slave makes. Flacus neatly brings each strap and clasp together and then, as usual, takes a step back in a humble posture.

Sertorius continues to watch him. »Why did you put the armor back on me?«, he asks, as harshly as he just commanded.

»Because you asked for it«, Flacus replies without hesitation.

»Yeahh«, says Sertorius, half to himself. »Go now! Get out!« With these words, he turns away from him, and goes to his chambers.

Flacus goes down to the slave barracks. For the next few hours, Sertorius will be occupied with his slave girls and will not need him.

»What happened?«, a familiar voice asks him in a whisper as the door of the barracks closes behind him.

»He wanted to know why I put the armor back on him.« The familiar voice asks no further; any more words would only be painful. He glances up the steps briefly. »Flacus, we will go tomorrow!«

»And Servilia?«

»We can't wait any longer. Praetorians will arrive in the next few days to guard the house. Sertorius is afraid.«

»Of whom?«

»Guess.«

*

Mirsa

»Cato, thank the gods, you are alive, come in.« With these words Sargon welcomes him, visibly pleased, yet depressed at the events of the past few weeks.

»They sat there as if they were longing for doom. A shadow of themselves«, Cato says in a feverish voice as he removes his breastplate.

»I know«, Sargon says in response, helping him take off his armor. »Sertorius?«, he then asks as Cato quiets down a bit.

»I've never seen him like he was in Asculum. It's more than just fear of losing goods, they fear doom.«

»They load ships in Ostia harbor, secretly of course, but I saw them. The streets lifeless, not only here. Rome equals a ghost town.«

»Yes«, Sargon replies, looking dejected in a way that is rarely seen in him.

»One more defeat and Crassus' army will also be beaten. What will we do then?«

»As I told you, Crassus has always seen himself in the shadow of Pompey. He will raise more troops, of that I am sure. Whether that will be enough, I don't know. The Thracian was about to escape with his people, over the Alps. His gladiators roughed up the whole Po Valley, but we wanted this to fail at all costs. Now half the Senate is sitting in Asculum trembling for its life.«

»Today it's you, who sounds like you hope they make it, across the Alps«, Cato says, but without reproach. »As I did, over a year ago, when I asked you about Thrajan.«

»Yes«, Sargon replies, briefly stroking his face with both hands as if to dispel worry. »As you see, age doesn't preserve one from helplessness or doubt.« He raises his head and lowers it again, as if searching for escaped thoughts. »The Senate is more than a somehow sensitive entity, always surrounded by new claims to power. We could have let the Thracian go. But in which direction would he turn? Would the insurrection collapse or strengthen? Which governors would we antagonize? An endless list of imponderables. So we hoped, believed, in the strength of our legions. And what no one thought possible has now happened. The Thracian remains victorious.«

Sargon pauses again. Cato watches him as he thinks with closed eyes, deep in thought, struggling with exhaustion, and again Cato catches himself wanting to ask him to rest, also because his lecture does not really hold anything new, but rejects this thought again, for it would only have the opposite effect. »So he's moving south again with his army«, Sargon continues. »The war continues on our soil. Supply, equipment for the troops, sun, rain, cold, all of this saps the strength and can wear down the strongest army. Here Crassus is superior to the Thracian and here time works for him. Perhaps there is still here and there a lucky coincidence, a mishap that helps him to the advantage. Even the Thracian is not invincible.« After a while he rises, slowly, like a tired bear. »Come, let's go outside to the porch«, he then says.

Both walk along the tablinum, then on through the large portico. Cato lets his eyes wander over the walls and ceilings and is pleased to see that everything is still as he remembers it. The marble steps worn, but still there.

The decorations fading, and yet he hasn't had them replaced. That's what he likes most about him, that things endure, in his world.

Both walk silently through the archway onto the porch, standing side by side they linger, looking at the lush plants. Sargon puts his hand on his shoulder. Cato looks at him, the old man's eyes are half closed, he seems lost in thought, a peaceful smile on his face.

»it all still appears as it was, like I saw it the last time, when I was here«, says Cato.

»Sounds to me you like it?«

»Yes.«

»Come, sit down«, Sargon adjusts his toga, and again there is a moment without anyone speaking. Cato is surrounded by a feeling of security and peace that he has only experienced in this house. He feels how much this longing for all the storms burned in him. Suddenly he thinks of Mirsa and fervently hopes that she, too, feels, has felt, similarly, in the rooms of this house. *Where might her house be, where is her home that fulfills all these longings? I never asked her about it.*

»What are you thinking?«, asks Sargon.

»Where was Mirsa's home?«

»She's from Syria.«

»I never asked her. You think she felt comfortable with us?«

»Cato, my dear, before we speak of her further - she is no longer with us.« Sargon looks into his nephew's questioning, startled eyes.

»She asked me to let her go to join the insurgents, and I gave her my ›yes‹ to it. Though asked her not to go, for of all the danger around, on that way there. But she left.

191

»And? Has she arrived?«

»I don't know.«

Both are silent thoughtfully.

Suddenly Jabulus appears. »Forgivness. Annaeus Serenus asks to be admitted.«

»At this hour? What can he want? He was at Asculum, wasn't he?«

»He was there«, says Cato, »but hardly spoke, unusual in him.«

Sargon tells Jabulus to invite him in and escort him to the entry hall

Dressed in white toga, the purple stripes on his tunic, and shoes of red leather, Annaeus appears on the steps leading down to the entry hall.

»Sargon.«

»Annaeus«, he returns the greeting, equally briefly.

»Marcus Licinius Crassus«, Annaeus begins in a sonorous voice, »went out with a formidable army against the insurgents and suffered defeat. I suppose details are unnecessary. The news runs through the country like wildfire. Fear is spreading like a virus. It has even infected our slave-flayer Cornelius.«

»In what way?« asks Sargon.

»His slaves, the ones that are left, gather his belongings. He doesn't think our troops will stop the Thracian, even if Mars himself were to lead them.«

»Cornelius. There you go.«

»He's not the only one, Sargon. What about you? What will you do?«

»What am I supposed to do? Who asks for it? I'm not one of the Aerarii Militaris. Why don't you talk to Sertorius?«

»Can't see it holds any meaning!«, replies Annaeus with a dismissive wave of his hand. »That an insurrection rages here has left the borders of the empire. If the Thracian remains victorious, tribes from the north will invade. To the east stand the hordes of Mithridates, who are marching more boldly than ever against Lucullus. The Thracian must fall, whatever the cost!«

»What are you thinking of?«, asks Sargon, impassively. Annaeus casts a glance at Cato.

»He may hear it«, says Sargon. »He hears everything that is spoken in this house.«

Annaeus hesitates. His forehead wrinkled, his left hand on the shoulder of his toga, he finally says: »The Cilicians must help us.«

Chapter 12.

Mons-Garganus

Tough and laborious have been the negotiations with the Cilicians. Although they may have been loose allies of the insurgents until now, they are not a solid people, divided, split into many clans that are always at odds, without any central authority that they follow in common.

Five hundred talents were paid and another one thousand is offered if they keep their agreement to stop supplying war equipment. Every senator, every nobleman, every citizen was reminded of his loyalty and love for the roman mother in order to raise the sum.

Tirelessly, the Senate advertised the advantage that would come along with it. The insurgents might continue to supply themselves with weapons from battles they had won, sufficient at the beginning of a insurrection, but too little for a long-lasting war. Shields and swords, taken from the enemy after battle, are rarely equal to new ones. Evading the enemy, searching for water, for camp site and supplies, hardly leave time to mend any pre-used.

*

When news of the successful negotiation with the Cilicians reaches Crassus, he sees himself forced into action.

›With great difficulty‹, he is told, ›the Senate has given him an advantage. And ›he must now end the war as

quickly as possible, since the Cilicians' promise is unlikely to last.‹

Enraged, he sends the couriers back to Rome, not without impressing upon them to admonish the Senate not to interfere in the future.

Compelled by the news, he forces the pursuit of the Thracian to the south. Knowing that the Thracian was moving along the coast, he ordered his troops to march west, along the foothills of the Apennines. Even if the baggage train lags behind, but it is the shorter way for his legions instead of following along the coast. Twice he forces the Thracian to battle, but cannot stop his advance. On a third attempt, in the northern lowlands of Mons-Garganus, he orders his troops to retreat quickly, expecting followed by the Thracian, yet his troops didn't take up any pursuit, which Crassus sees as possible evidence of the Cilician's lack of weapons supplies.

He waits until they have left the lowlands and reached the narrow breach between the foothills of Mons-Garganus and the Apennines. Here he pushes for a decisive battle.

As the insurgents appears on the horizon, he forms his legions in the shape of a crescent, the opening facing away from the enemy, and the outer legions of the bend, in the scars of the rocky landscape. Then he waits, till the first lines at the centre are colliding and orders then the outer ones to swing forward, occupying the slightly rising terrain and thus strengthening the encirclement. But, *wrath of the Gods*, the Thracian seems to have succeeded overnight in sending thousands to the rocks above him, who now shower his legions with a hail of stones.

Horrified is Crassus forced to watch as his army is pushed back, thus opening the way to the south. *Suspected*, Crassus thinks, *he suspected it, that's why he didn't pursue us, but sent his men ahead.*

Only the death count allows him to write reassuring to the Senate:

> insurgents with great losses
> Shield only rarely among the fallen.
> Tribute to the Cilicians seems to pay off.

*

The winter is unusually cold. Heavy rains and snowfalls force both armies to stay in their camps. After several weeks of gruelling mutual siege, unexpected news reaches the Roman camp:

> Today, early evening.
> Thracian marches most of the women
> and children to the sea
> Accompaniment: four legions.

Again, it is the Cilicians who help them to their advantage, this time by sending a message. There is talk of a large sum, and the Cilicians must also hand over hostages to the Thracian. Crassus consults briefly with his officers. The pirate rabble works to both sides, this was to be expected. So there is little doubt about the scouts' report, also since they speak of large troop movements. They swiftly agree that this must be an act of desperation, if the Thracian tries to hand over his people to the Cilicians, despite the dangers.

Crassus has the army form up and in rapid marches they move under storm and hail to Mons-Garganus.

A terrible killing begins. Crassus, knowing the circumstances of the enemy, wants the decision today. Unyielding he drives his legions into battle, despite the dangers of the tempest.

Victory seems within reach, when suddenly another enemy appears in the rear. The four legions that had marched to the sea have returned, prudent enough not to take the same path. Fiercely the battle continues, still the falling darkness forces the two armies apart.

Even if it is not a defeat, the losses on the side of the insurgents are enormous and many have fallen into Roman captivity. At midnight, the first scouting parties return with the news that four thousand dead have been counted and about twice as many wounded. Among the slaves, however, twelve thousand dead. A great victory, even if a few thousand of their own ranks became prisoners. Crassus hides his joy at this news, no expression, nor mimic or gestures, betrays it .»How is young Cato?«, he asks briefly, since he hasn't turned up.

»He's one of the prisoners«, the legate replies.

»Are you sure?«

»Yes. We talked to some men who saw him fall into the hands of the insurgents.«

On the next day Crassus sends two couriers to Rome with the request to the Senate to provide him with the Quaestor Scrofa. The latter is to raise at least three legions and move

south with them to the vicinity of Nuceria and stay there until he receives word from him.

He tries to contact the Cilicians again about the sudden tur-naround of the insurgents who had marched to the sea, but can only get vague information.

But this is not a cause for concern, because apart from the victory, the last events brought to light something that neither he, nor his officers, have paid attention to so far: Women and children the Thracian wanted to hand over to the Cilicians. He carries women and children with him, a disadvantage they will exploit from now on.

*

Cato opens his eyes, tries to raise his head, but it hurts too much. He looks around. A few torches light up the room. Then he hears some flapping sounds, like from a tent canvas. *A tent, then, I'm lying in a tent*. Effortly, he turns his head aside. A face bends over him, Mirsa. He wants to say something, but she gently puts her hand over his mouth, then gives him some-thing to drink. »You have a wound on your head«, she then says, »and your leg is broken, we have splinted it. You are one of our prisoners, yet nothing to fear. They will trade you. Pro-bably as early as tomorrow night.«

Cato lies back, feels miserable and weak. »How did you find me«, he then brings through between his teeth still.

»When they captured you, they asked you for your name. You may not remember. And there are the other

prisoners of Crassus' army. They were forced to give an-swers, I know too little about that.

But our heralds eventually went through our camp asking for those who escaped from your house, the house of Sargen, that's how they found me.«

»Are we here in your camp?«

»Yes, we are south of the Mons-Garganus. Crassus is only a day's march away. But it's been raining and storming for days.«

»South of the Mons-Garganus«, Cato repeats silently, over and over, as if he had to guess the meaning. He puts his head aside and looks at Mirsa. A few months ago, she received him as a slave in his uncles house. She has always been there. He has known her since he was a child. Yet today he wakes up in a tent, in the camp of the insurgents, wounded, and she tends to his wounds. Her face, so familiar and yet so foreign. Her features have changed.

The childishly shy smile has given way to a woman's face. She puts the jug aside and sits down next to him.

»Long before you leaft our house, they tried to escape across the Alps«, Cato tries to tie in, to the bond that had been between them both.

»Yes.«

»What happened?« he asks her.

»They had almost reached them, but your legions, - they had to fight, again and again. They defeated them, but - the supplies were then depleted, and in the mountains the children would have died first.«

The tent entrance opens and five men come in. All of tall stature, with black, shoulder-length, tousled hair.

They exchange a few words with Mirsa, which he doesn't understand, and glance at him with glowing eyes. Eyes of hunted animals, driven by fear and hate and despair. *These men are here because of me*. He tries to repeat this thought, to hold it, but it mingles with the memory of his return from

Alexandria, the day of the auction, the man in Flavius' house, the 'I', how much fear, hatred, despair it can ingest, keep away, endure. He feels heat in his temples, his pulse hammering, believes the pulse suddenly quickening, intensifying the feeling of heat in his temples.

»They know about you«, he then hears Mirsa's voice again, »also that you are a legate in Crassus' army. They want to ask you some questions. I will translate it.«

»I will try to answer as best I can.«

»Why didn't you let us go, over the Alps?«, she asks him.

»I don't know.«

Mirsa translates briefly. The man speaks again, softly, almost in a whisper, choppy, struggling to control himself, with the voice of the desperate.

»He wants to know what you believe yourself. You must have known that you wouldn't have been able to defeat us back then. That we are forced then to move south again, - and yet you did everything to prevent our escape across the Alps.«

Cato listens to her, hears her trembling voice. *What to answer?*, he asks himself. Telling her that which must not, can not be? Tell her that Rome will never allow tens of thousands of slaves to gain their freedom by crushing Roman legions?

»It's politics. It's the Senate, intrigue and scheming for power«, he briefly skims his words and adds, »I'm afraid I can't give you a better answer. I have never been a senator, nor have I ever been fond of politics. I was in Alexandria for a long time and with the study of philosophers....«, *What am I talking...what's wrong with you?*, and breaks off.

Mirsa translates and the men confer briefly. Cato listens and tries to pick up the sound of the voices, but the thundering tent canvas swallows most of it. Suddenly, the tent entrance opens again. A courier peeks in briefly and delivers a message, it seems. He tries to straighten up a bit to get a better view of what is happening. One of the men comes closer. For the first time he can see the face clearly, the features seem hardened. The gaze is straight and penetrating. He speaks to Mirsa without taking his eyes off Cato.

»A man of spirit«, Mirsa translates, »and yet you are in the Roman army?«

Cato does not believe that this is really surprising. His reaction to the question they want to see, they want to read.

»I am there as a legate«, he looks at the faces and feels that this is not enough. »Crassus belongs to those whom we call optimates. They are advocates of the supremacy of the nobility. I belong to the Populars. It is important for us to know what decisions he makes, inside and outside the army«, here he breaks off again, realizing again of not being able to keep track of his sentences. Listening, speaking, - all difficult. His head hurts and his leg sends waves of pain through his body with every movement.

»Do you think that Crassus, - would negotiate with us?«, asks Mirsa, carefully bringing out each word.

Cato gazes the round, looking at the tense faces. There they stand, undoubtedly the leaders of the insurrection, the victors in this two-year battle with Roman legions. And even though they may be completely indifferent to these victories, this question must still hurt. For it can only lead to ask -Them-, the former tormentors. He hesitates, the words get stuck in his throat, moves his head then, gently, negating her question. »No«, he then says with certainty. »Crassus is corroded of ambition. He left no stone unturned to gain command of the troops.« He waits for a question to follow, but the men remain silent, waiting in turn to see if he will continue.

»We could also leave the country by ships«, Mirsa says into the silence, as if to erase this moment so that it would not give birth to its to his misfortune. »A city smaller than Naples. A city we don't have to spend months besieging. We can't trust the Cilicians, they don't want us to leave the country any more than you do. They would betray us.«

»In Velia you might find ships, even men skilled in shipbuilding. A city in Lucania. on the west coast, far south of Naples.« »We would have to cross the Apennines again, and building ships takes time. We need a city, with a number of ships that can hold our army.«

»I, - I don't know of any, - don't know of any city, any town, that might have that.«

Another day as prisoner passes for Cato, Mirsa takes care of him. The pain subsides, but it continues to rob him of sleep. On the day Mirsa lets him know that the exchange with Crassus is imminent, he holds her back by her arm and asks her a question that has suddenly seized him: »Why ar you releasing me? Aren't you afraid that I might tell of your plans to get you ships? Why did you let me know this?«

»We cannot spread the search for such a city in the camp, so we had to ask you. But most of all, - we're not as strong as we were at the beginning. Many of our men were taken captive in the last battle. You are very important to the Romans. They were willing to release 500 of our men. And there, - of course, - we said yes. If you had named a city, there wouldn't be an exchange«, a little startled by her words, she adds: »There wouldn't be one tomorrow, but surely in a few more days or weeks, when we were close to that city. I have to go«, and slips outside through the tent entrance. Cato stays behind alone. A tangle of questions and possibilities floods his brain. How can I keep it quiet, postpone the exchange, not postpone ... get to Rome .... talk to Sargon....you can't side with them.

*

On wooden wagons the prisoners of the last battle are brought to Rome. Once there, they are chained together, whether they are children, women or men. In a long line they are led through Rome towards the Field of Mars. No method of humiliation, no matter how ghastly, is left out. The crowd is hysterical. After months of fear, darkly repressed doubts, the certainty must return, needs to flood everything, shall leave nothing that could shake the attitude that those there are the slaves and they the dominators. One wants to feel the Roman order again. To feel that this is the world. They are kicked and spat upon, faeces are poured out over them. Women are groped and fingered in all regions of their bodies, because the returning certainty must be palpable, must be tangible.

Nauseated, Sargon turns away and walks down the street. Cato was wounded in the last battle and was taken prisoner, according to the latest reports. He hopes for messengers with new news, but in vain. So he gets back on the wagon and re turns to his house. There he is already awaited by an uninvited guest, Sertorius.

Sertorius considered it appropriate to be present, when the prisoners arrived in Rome. Also to visit Sargon. Like the latter, he hopes to hear from Cato, though less concerning his health than on developments on the battlefield.

»Sertorius, - unannounced as usual. What brings you to me?«, Sargon greets him.

»Your hospitality cannot be surpassed!«

»My way passed over the Mars-Field. Yours?«

»Also!«, replies Sertorius briefly, demanding. Knowing this won't be all.

»Go on! Did I miss something!«

»Possibly. Did you blindfold yourself and let yourself be led like a blind man?«

»No«, replies Sertorius, with his characteristic provocative tone, »but I saw nothing that deserved special attention.«

»No doubt at all«, Sargon replies in a bristling voice.

»I saw slaves«, Sertorius presses out between his teeth and takes a step toward him. »Slaves who dared to take up the sword against their masters, who were defeated by our troops and brought back to receive their just punishment. What did you see?«

»I saw men and women and children«, Sargon replies, »most shamefully abused.«

»What is that talk that you're spouting. Isn't Cato, your nephew, schooled in Alexandria?«

»That's the way it is.«

»Then teach me now. As it says in the writings of Aristotle:

›Wherever one is composed of several and a common one arises, either from continuous or separate parts there …‹ «,

Sertorius stops, for Sargon interrupts him, ties in the sentence: »›… there will be a dominant and a ruled one. Namely this is found in ensouled living beings on the basis of their entire nature.«

»Well then!«, Sertorius continues, demanding, »then we're agreed!«, and pretends to be waiting for Sargon to answer, but only briefly, only formally. »These are the maxims of our state, our empire«, he then quickly continues, in order to smother every word that might still form in Sargon's mouth. »Our entire culture is based on these considerations. There is no reason to doubt it, and there will be none«, and falls back into raging rage, ready to crush anything and anyone, wherever it dares to raise opposition. »Everything must be done to prevent the Thracian with his heap of slaves, by whatever means, from leaving the country. Our legions will destroy those who are meant to be dominated, 'till is nothing left.«

»Because they are slaves, tools, animated possessions?«

»Quite so. that's right«, Sertorius rages on. »I advise you, Sargon, to learn this formula quickly again.« With these words he squeezes himself into his breastplate and leaves the house without any sort of goodbye.

Chapter 13.

Twelve Legions

Deep black night, men come into the tent. They put Cato on a stretcher, while outside a large group of horsemen and foot soldiers is waiting to join them. No one speaks with him, but he senses the imminent exchange. After hours the two enemy troops come closer, surrounding each other, sneaking around, each side worried about losing the pledge.

Cato feels feverish, his eyes glowing, suddenly he believes the exchange has failed, believes himself on his way back to the insurgents' camp, then confusion again. Endless waves between fever-distorted voices and images. The heat in his body finally seems to be fading. He feels the cool morning wind on his face, opens his heavy lids and let his eyes follow the wispy clouds above him, until he remembers his situation, yet memories of the exchange remain absent. Unable to manage a glimp over the edge of the wagon, but his uncertainty subsides when he notices the familiar sound of marching roman legionnaires.

*

Sargon walks down the hall to the dining room to check on Cato. The wounds have healed well, he will be on his way again soon. As he enters the hall, a servant of the house is removing the midday meal, and he sits down with him. Thus they spend a while without speaking, each glad of the other's company.

»Mirsa is with them?« Sargon asks in a low, calm voice.

»Yes. She's fine, I think«, Cato continues, realizing that through his silence, Sargon is cautiously asking him to say more: »They all seemed very distressed. They asked me why we didn't let them go when they were at the foot of the Alps.«

»And? What did you tell them?«

»Me? – What should I have told them? The questions came from five men, Mirsa translated. One of them may have been the leader, the Thracian, Spartacus. I'm not sure. Their hatred of us - they seemed to, - they did'nt know where to go, how to turn, not knowing a way out, what else to... I was afraid to tell them that Rome will never allow slaves to leave this country, will never let that happen, after they ...«

»Yes - I see«, says Sargon.

»Mirsa suddenly said, almost pleading, they could also leave the country with ships. And I answered that they can find ships in Velia, even sailors know about shipbuilding.« He pauses as the events replay over and over in his mind. Then hopes for a few words from his uncle, but Sargon remains silent, only his facial expressions, his posture, betray strained thought. »Crassus knows nothing of this«, he therefore continues. »He was with me briefly, asking about my condition, but I told him nothing about Velia.«

Sargon listens attentively. Sunk into himself, he replies:

»Cato, my dear, you must leave this very day and return to the army.«

»He doesn't know, and he never has to know.«

»He'll probably never know, not really. But he will learn that the Thracian was called a city. And then? Who was it? Who could it have been? To be able to suddenly name a traitor, to blame someone for the failure of the legions, for the shameful defeats, Crassus can't get past that, even if he wanted to. This is then also fuelled by others. You've been in the insurgents' camp, it's possible to suspect you, it's imposing itself. They will suspect all of us, the family of the Sargen. This long-lasting, disgraceful war against slaves, it touches the pillars. You understand?«

»Yes«, Cato replies, and his voice reveals his unwillingness to bow to the facts.

»Can you ride?«, he then asks him. »Does it go already, with the leg?«

»Yes.«

»Tell him as soon as you get back to camp! Don't wait 'till he calls for you. That way he can deal with your supposed betrayal as if you had acted in threatening circumstances.«

Towards evening Cato gets ready to leave, Sargon accompanies him to the gate. A slave of the house leads Cato's horse.

»Take this dagger. Take it!«, says Sargon a little more sternly than usual.

»What for?«

»Should something happen to you, should you find yourself on the battlefield with a mortal wound, take the dagger, don't wait for vultures and jackals to bite you to death.«

They both hug each other goodbye. »And the gods«, Sargon adds some final words, »if they exist, may they be with you.«

*

On bad roads Cato rides back to the roman army under the protection of an escort. The Centurions are silent, the legionnaires no less so. He, too, feels no urge for long-winded conversations. When they set up camp in the evening, he usually retreats. Now and then he can pick up a thread of conversation. There is talk of changeful battles. The Quaestor Scrofa had arrived at some point in the rear of the insurgents. The Thracian focused all his forces on him, the breakthrough would probably have succeeded, ›but... a bridge... Scrofa has torn it down‹, so it sounded, right after he had crossed it. Risky for himself, but he knew Crassus was nearby. ›The Thracian then fled eastward with his troops. The legions pursued them, driving them before them‹, one said. ›Then finally they could be placed, but ...‹ *How it went on, I'll find out in the camp*, Cato thinks. *They didn't defeat him, that much is certain.*

Strenuous it goes on, over the passes of the Apennines. They ride until late at night. Then, finally, standing on the crest of a hill, they see the camp in the distance, lit by torchlight.

A brief exchange with the guards at the Decumanic Gate while allowing them to pass.

The camp itself still seems alive despite the late hour. Swords are being sharpened, shields mended, tents under construction. Smaller detachments move through the tent cities, led by Centurions giving their instructions.

Tired from the exertions of the last days, Cato rides to the officers' tent city. On the other side of the path Drusus comes towards him, he seems to be in a hurry. Cato's still calling for him. He has had many conversations with him since he served as a legate in the roman army, and Drusus is very open-minded. When Cato has questions about the latest events or the next steps, he trusts him the most.

»You are in a hurry, I see. Just tell me what happened. The escort spoke of heavy fighting and Scrofa had arrived. The Thracian fled east with his army, that's all I know.«

»They fled east, back to their camp«, we thought. But then we faced them in the bend of the river. You remember, the river, south of Mons-Garganus. So we could not take advantage of our superiority in numbers. Of course, we fought them, but they escaped across the rIver, quickly, very quickly. They must have had boats with them, rafts too.«

»The Cilicians?«

»No, I don't think so. In their camp we found tools, also half-finished scaffolding.«

Cato feels an icy shudder when Drusus speaks of boats, because he hears Mirsa's voice: ›We could also use ships...‹, but he tells him nothing about it. Though he trusts him, Drusus is a roman officer through and through. »You assign the guards?«, Cato asks instead.

»Yes.«

»Then I shall sleep well.«

»You can«, Drusus says in response as he puts on his helmet. »Don't be troubled. Twelve legions lie here.«

Twelve legions Cato repeats in his mind, *twelve legions we need.*

*

With an icy face, not looking at him, Crassus accepts Cato's report. »I could have you chained after your treachery«, and stares at him for a while. Finally he calls a Centurion and give order to send two couriers to Rome at once, accompanied by three hundred horsemen, with the message to immediately send sailors to Velia, to pull the ships out of the port. »What happens to you at next«, he turns to Cato again, in a somber voice that can mean many things, »You stay in the camp!«

Supplying the troops is more difficult than Crassus expected, but the enemy is worse off, of that he is certain. Once again the signal of the guards rings, horsemen return from their scouting party. Crassus rides to the Praetorian Gate, Scrofa behind him and calls for the Centurion to report him.

In brief words, he informs him that the insurgents are moving south-west in forced marches, despite the snow and cold. Crassus thinks for a moment, wants to send them out again, but commands then the Centurion to leave. He wants to give his legions one more day of rest and then follow the Thracian.

»He won't take a detour«, he turns to Scrofa. »Straight to Velia, that's the way he takes.«

»What about us?«, Scrofa asks after a moment's hesitation, but irrelevantly, without attaching any weight to the question. The certainty of the strength of their legions has grown with the victory and with it the confidence to finally crush the slave army.

»They can't take a city like Velia in one day. We'll send a squad of horsemen to Velia, they should get there before the insurgents. They will convey to the city fathers that we are following in the enemy's rear and that Velia is to be held until we arrive.«

»We can't keep them waiting too long.«

»Neither shall we, but four or five days they have to withstand. Maybe that's not even necessary. Tomorrow you will follow the Thracian. You will receive eight of our legions. Go after him, disturb the rearguard if you can, but I expressly comand you to not engage him. I'll move with the rest of our armee to Nola for further recruitments. Many won't be, but they'll make up for the losses from the last battle. In four days, we'll be able to join you again. The Thracian has lost his nimbus and I don't think he will have much inflow on the road to Velia. We will outnumber him three to one. It will be decided in Velia. The decision falls in Velia«

He dismisses Scrofa and rides through the camp, closely followed by his bodyguard. As he nears his tent, one of his officers is already waiting for him, a scroll of papyrus in his hand. It is Cinnas, one of those who already belonged to his inner circle under Sulla.

Crassus exchanges a glance with him, then motions for the bodyguards to stay back. »So?«, he then asks.

»Read it! Found on Cato, your legate.«

He follows Cinnas' hand to a marked spot. »There's no place for such spirits here!«, Cinnas continues, as Crassus just gives him a questioning angry look.

»Let's go in the tent«, Crassus says upon and waves the guards to open the entry. Still while they both move in Crassus takes the papyrus from his hand, waits then 'till the guards close the entry again and reads the lines silently, just for himself:

›God created everyone free.
Nature made no one a slave.
Alkidamas of Elijah.'

»Alkidamas of Elijah, philosopher, lived about 200 years ago«, he then says to Cinnas and gives him the papyrus back.

» ›For the like is tribal to the like by nature‹ «,

Cinnas reads on where Crassus broke off,

» ›but custom, the tyrant of men,

enforces many things against nature.‹ «

»Hippias of Elis«, Crassus answers his questioning gaze, »lived more than 300 years ago.«

»I was sure, that you would know even this one. - The custom, the tyrant of men? Isn't that enough for you!? Isn't it enough to recognize him, this Cato, for what he is!? Do you know how we buried Sulla or your father? - Forcing someone like you into court, there are customs even there. How many of our laws are based on or preserve customs? To preserve them, that's what we go to battle for...«

»Stop it! What' you want! Teach me!?«, Crassus hisses at him.

»Send him away!«

»No!«, Crassus says firmly.

»You want to keep using him as your legate?«

»He has reported to the Senate impeccably so far, and he will continue to do so.«

»How? In the name of ONE God who created all free? We implore THE GODS for help, Zeus, Apollo, Mars ...«

»Oh really!?«, Crassus sharply cuts him short, has further words on his lips already, but holds back at first, has a damp cloth handed to him instead, and rubs the dust from his face.

»I find these thoughts as dangerous as all of you. But look at your legionnaires, and then look at this Cato. He is young, a philosopher, an idealist. He will continue to brief the Senate, and will be more conscientious and careful in doing so than anyone else. And you know why? Because he wants to know how much truth there is, in those words he found somewhere along the way. And because of _be_cause_ that is so«, Crassus goes on, setting each word like a sword thrust, »he will tell us, we will know through him whether we have conquered.

»You need a philosopher to know if we've won...«

»Who allows you to speak like that!? Questioning me like that!?«

»You do. Always have.«

»And? Have you ever served under a Consul and experienced the like? – How!?«, Crassus goes on, but his tone has changed, from harsh, angry, to matter-of-fact and critical.

»How should I know, about the state of our troops, about your loyalty, if I wouldn't let you speak. Do you understand now!? Who better than this Cato could tell us whether we have won? DE-FEATED what is fighting us there. That Thracian out there isn't just any insurrection.« Crassus pauses, suddenly remembering his quarrel with Annaeus, more than seven months ago, where he used the same sentence. Instantly, philosophy storms his brain, tortures him with questions about the meaning of this repetition, floods his mind with reflections of the moving and the immovable, the heaviness and the weightless, each with different characteristics, and thus also the being, the states of being. *My state*, he thinks *my state*. With an abrupt twist of his body, he tears himself away from the thoughts.

»And you want me to send him away!?«, he continues,

»Why!? Out of fear!? Fear of whom!? Of what!? Mars and Apoll are on our side, Cinnas!? Aren't they?! See, that's wha this war is about. That's what it's all about. And that's why he's staying!«

Cinnas grabs his helmet without further ado and leaves with the usual gesture, but without a word. At the tent exit, he turns around once more. »Is it him or is it you who digs for this truth?«

*

While Scrofa pursues the Thracian, Crassus reaches the city of Nola. After a short time, more troops are ready to march off, for he forced the city fathers to recruit, threatening them with severe reprisals should they falter in their loyalty to the roman mother.

*

Slave girls

There they lie, the two bodies, still twitching with pain, unable to get up on their own. Somewhat apart, huddles, sobbing again and again, sits Tiberius. *Oh, for God's sake, I didn't mean to.*

Why am I so punished? – Though he wanted, wanted to touch women's bodies again. Drunk by the sexual pleasures of others, he believed it would be possible today, yet everything remained flabby at him. But it shouldn't be his fault. No, it wasn't his fault! These women, these young women. While they strived with his penis, he clearly saw the giggles on their faces. It was their fault and if they are guilty, they must be beaten too! His eyes wander again over the wounds of the bodies lying naked before him. The abdomen of the petite woman seems to swell. Finally, two servants of the house come and lay her on a stretcher. They ask questions, which Tiberius does not answer. Motionless he sits there and lets everything happen around him apathetically. May they ask, he will not give them an answer. *What do these creatures know*, he thinks to himself. *Don't stare at me so brazenly, or you'll be the next to be put on the stretcher. They are slaves, slave girls, like those sold by the hundreds in the markets every day*. But here the thread, on which this stream of thought has snaked along, breaks, and drowns in the feeling of hatred, bitterness, and tormenting shame before himself. Slowly, with a deep sigh, he rises and leaves the room. Slightly bent over, he stops and leans against one of the pillars. Again a deep sigh comes out of him, because the feeling of... he is unable to recognize, not any color of it, only annoying discomfort, when suddenly a hand comes to his arm. Startled, he looks into the face of his steward.

»You look tired, you should rest.«

»Aah! Get away!«, unwilling he pushes his hand aside.

»I have good news of Crassus' army movements. He has pushed the slaves south, near the city of Velia. We could leave for your country seat in Lucania today. After such a long time, this would certainly be a welcome recovery.« Tiberius looks doubtfully at his steward, but his eyes are already glowing with joyful anticipation.

»Crassus has weakened them decisively before, at Mons Garganus, as you will recall. And he has been able to strengthen his army even more. There's nothing to worry about.«

»Yes, of course. You're right«, Tiberius replies in a soft tone, and a tremor runs through his body. »Tell our people to prepare everything.« Full of longing for the only place where his bodily desires can experience refreshment, he sets off with his entourage, thinking of his 'little fish'.

*

Scrofa

Already a few days after the separation from the main army, Scrofa with his eight legions has caught up with the insurgents on their way south, and, in various ways, as ordered by Crassus, hinders their advance. Again and again he attacks the rearguard and achieves slight successes. Prisoners are crucified, on the trees along the roads.

When they come near the river Casuentus, whose banks are flooded, preventing the insurgents from advancing, the officers urge their Quaestor to seize the opportunity to lead them against the Thracians once and for all, and promise a brilliant victory in the name of the legions.

Scrofa hesitates, finally gives in to the urge and calls the troops into battle formation. After an hour, he regrets it. For his troops, just demanding battle before, turn to flee, in wild panic, throwing shields and swords away, unable to face the wounded, irascible beast that suddenly confronts them, to tear apart their pursuers with all fury and despair.

Scrofa sends couriers to Crassus to come to his aid, and tries in vain to stop the fleeing troops.

When Crassus reaches his demoralized army and learns of the ignominious escape of his legionnaires, he furiously decides on one of the cruellest punishments in the roman army system. That very evening he announces his decision to the commanders of his legions. »Hear me. The last battle was lost because our legionnaires were deserted by the virtue of valor but afflicted by cowardice. This disease also occurred in earlier days, and our forefathers felt compelled to resort to a curative remedy in the name of Rome. And so I hereby order a

decimation; the death of every tenth combatant. Lots will decide who it will strike and who will be spared.«

»Crassus, you mustn't do that«, they urge him immediately, with uncontrollable horror barely after he has ended. »There hasn't been a decimation for more than a hundred years, not even Sulla has resorted to this barbaric means.«

»By all the gods!? Are you about to tell me what is lawful for me?«, he angrily rules them. »The Senate gave me all the powers! And as I say, it shall be done!«

Scrofa also presses him, almost pleads, not to impose such a cruel punishment in anger, since many patricians also fought in those ranks. Yet Crassus cannot be dissuaded from this desicion by no matter how they are pleading him.

While the dispersed troops gradually rejoin the army, news of the decimation rushes to Rome. The nobility is outraged, but the Senate keeps a low profile and has no intention of interfering. »If it brings back discipline ...«, is the only verbal utterance before it shuts itself off completely from the nobility and the public.

The nobility suspects the closest relatives in the ranks of the condemned. In desperation, many set out the same day, despite the dangers, to shut off this barbaric act.

When Crassus learns of this, he hastily takes the necessary measures to execute the sentence and sends a cohort to intercept the nobility by force, if necessary, and to admonish them not to exhibit before all the world, through their clumsy behaviour, what shameful measures they are forced to take.

Then he has the centre of the camp prepared to have the execution visible to all. Five hundred men, those who fled most shamefully, are brought in. Divided into fifty sections of ten each. Whom the lot meets, shall be chastised with rods to the flesh and executed afterwards.

*

There will be no more ships in Velia, so the Thracian drives his army further south, Crassus follows him relentlessly.

On the mountainsides of the Apennines, the terrain is often sloping, the nights cold and rainy, the roads washed out or covered with mud, skirmishes with the rearguard again and again. But Crassus' legions, after the implemented decimation, endure the hardships without contradiction.

After weeks of tenacious persecution, at last seems an opportunity to force the Thracian for battle.

»Forgive me, Consul. I would never dare to enter without permission. But our scouts report that while crossing the river, the bridges were suddenly swept away by the waters, part of the slave army had to stay behind.«

Crassus does not hesitate, he immediately orders the troops to assemble, leads them through the valley and drives them into battle. When they finally succeed in encircling the insurgents, the trombones announce the approach of a new enemy. Faster than expected, the Thracian has led his troops back across the river, to help his own.

Crassus looks west. The sun is low. Long shadows under a reddish horizon, on which a black, flickering line suddenly appears. In long-drawn battle line, fast like hungry wolves, the enemy troops storm.

Crassus hastily pulls his legions together and turns them toward this further enemy, extending the frontline to avoid being surrounded himself.

Already all tactics, all calculations seem to be in vain, the two armies collide terribly.

Crassus surrenders the first two legions, but unlike in previous battles, he remains calm, his numerical superiority gives him security. Coolly, he lets the rear legions form up and extends the battle line once again, knowing that the Thracian cannot oppose him.

Again it is the falling darkness that forces the two armies apart.

Chapter 14.

Negotiations

More than a year has passed since Crassus led the roman legions against the Thracian. Five times he has fought against him, without being able to give a turn to the war. Forceful was his speech to the senators. Six weeks, three months at the most, that's all he, Crassus, would need to wear down the 'riff-raff'.

A series of demands he had imposed on the Senate before agreeing to accept the supreme command of the troops. His conditions were accepted, but his real aim, to finally crown himself with the laurel wreath of the commander and to enter Rome like Pompeius Magnus to the cheers of the masses, has failed.

No matter the outcome of the war, in the eyes of the Romans, it will have taken too long to overthrow an army of slaves.

*

six thousand eight hundred

Sertorius is left alone. Awkwardly he rolls up the courier's report. A report written by Cato. *By Cato*, he thinks, *schooled in Alexandria, how can he write like that. ...our legions, undefeated throughout the empire, have been fighting the rabble for nearly three years.... in our own country...they are nothing but vermin...what shame, what disgrace....*

He unrolls the report to read again. And reads silently. Shifts the papyrus, turns it as if searching the lines, for more lines, in the lines for what is hidden. Hoping for words that, content or statement, change:

> ...in the last battle, on the side of the slaves,
>
> two out of six thousand eight hundred
>
> wounded in the back, the others died
>
> their faces turned to the enemy.

How much longer, thinks Sertorius. How long will the Thracian last? Will new slaves join him again?... the Cilicians, will they supply him with weapons again? Why does Crassus not succeed? Why he can't crush the rebellion? Endless tormenting questions that gag the day, the weeks and the months.

*

we'll fight

As Cato leaves the tent that morning, he sees a group of horsemen leaving the camp at the Praetorian Gate, numbering at least one cohort. By his helmet and armor he recognizes a Centurion who is just stepping out of one of the opposite tents.

»They want to negotiate with the insurgents, that's all I know.«

Cato gets on his horse and rides through the camp. He just manages to stop Drusus, who is hastily trying to catch up.

»The Senate is considering summoning Lucullus or Pompey. If this happens and they intervene in the war, the crushing of the slave army will be attributed to them. Crassus fears to be deprived of victory.«

»And now he wants to negotiate?«, asks Cato. »About what? What does he want to offer them?«

»I don't know. I have to go on«, Drusus replies, pushing his spurs into the horse's sides.

*

In the distance, amidst the parched land, a misty, hazy cloud looms. For a group of Romans, led by Crassus, it seems to stand still at first. But after a while there is no doubt, flying up dusty sand, stirred up by the riders of the insurgents, among them the Thracian Spartacus, with whom a meeting has been arranged.

Crassus rides with his men to the centre of a flat elevation, which stands out from the rest of the desolation with its bare, yellow sandy ground and can be easily seen on all sides.

He calls the Centurions to line up in two rows. Then he orders the older ones, including Cinnas, to the front, the younger ones, like Drusus, to the second row. He quickly turns forward again to hide his shudder, for the image of the young Drusus, who is looking forward spellbound remains in him.

The enemy horsemen are approaching, *eight or ten* thinks Crassus, then they disappear in a depression and again only a cloud of dust is visible to the Romans.

Tensely they stare at the ridge in front of them, where the horde of enemy horsemen is about to appear, their faces will then be recognizable.

The enemy horsemen are approaching, Crassus estimates them at eight or ten. A valley depression takes the view, and again the Romans are left only with the swirling, dusty sand.

Tensely they stare at the ridge in front of them, where the horde of enemy horsemen is about to appear, their faces will then be recognizable.

Crassus feels his pulse up to his temples. Finally he will get to see the Thracian, the leader. He wants to see, wants to know at last, if there is something about this man, a hint, a mark, a Somehow-Somewhat, that distinguishes him from other slaves. This, he hopes, would end roiling questions, restless thinking through what is happening.

At a measured distance, forming a line, the enemy horsemen stop in front of him and his companions. Crassus settles on the man in the middle because it would be the usual formation, and only he appears in thracian armor. He examines the outer appearance. Dark hair appears on the sides of the helmet, which seems to hide a high forehead. Scars cover the muscular, long arms. Then he tries to catch the other's gaze. The Thracian seems to be looking at him and through him at the same time. Crassus raises his right hand in greeting: »I greet the leader of the brave gladiator army.«

Surprised, absorbing deep the cold air, Drusus observes what is happening. Not the Thracian but Crassus, supreme general of the Republic, greets first. His gaze rests tensely on the thracian and his men, waiting for their reaction. As they do not respond, Drusus takes this venture as already failed. Never before have there been negotiations between commanders of roman legions and rebellious escaped slaves. The special circumstances, the over two years lasting victory of this Thracian and the almost sick ambition of his commander, have made this meeting come about. Then his breath catches again. The man to the left of the Thracian translates the greeting into a language that is foreign to him. Drusus tosses his head to the right, just for a moment to read the faces of the others. With excessive discipline, concealing their insecurity, they look upon the enemy. But their frozen posture leaves no doubt. Again he hears that foreign accent, the man on the left returns the greeting. *How does he manage to have his men fight us so fiercely, so determinedly, so bravely? Defeating us in our own country time and time again for almost three years, when he doesn't even speak the only language which is understandable by every ethnic group in his army.* As a boy he often listened to the war-reports. There was talk always, of commanders who cheered their men on, spoke to them, encouraged them and formed them into a sworn community, his search for this was in vain. The roman army is a tightly organized machinery in every detail, in which there is no place for general-soldier war romance. But there, opposite him, stands the Thracian, leader of an army of runaway slaves and gladiators, which seems to unite all this in themselves.

Drusus awakens from his milling thinking, again he hears the voice of the translator. He asks to be let go, to a city on the west coast, with a sufficient number of ships to return to their countries.

»Marcus Licinius Crassus, supreme commander of the Republic, speaks to you«, Crassus harshly interrupts the translator.

»on behalf of the roman Senate, I have the following offer. You and a hundred of your men, the choice is yours, will be granted freedom! The rest surrender at the mercy or mercilessness of the Senate.« Again, he seeks the Thracian's gaze as he speaks to the man on his left and lets him translate.

Drusus looks at the translator's facial features. Evenly they run across forehead, nose and chin. Fleshy cheeks, dark eyes above, deep in their sockets. He's noticing the pronunciation. It may have a foreign accent, but this is the sound of the philosophers, the thinkers.

»We were slaves because you made us, not because we are«, the translator continues.

»You are slaves and will remain so and perish on the battlefield«, replied Crassus.

The translator passes on Crassus' words without taking his eyes off him. Then he falls silent. Tense silence now. Motionless, both sides look at each other.

»We are only concerned with your attitude toward slavery«, the translator suddenly continues, »to the extent that it is one of the reasons you are here today. You wouldn't have come to negotiate with slaves, unless Pompey had been asked by the Senate, - to help you.«

Crassus grabs the reins of his horse tighter instantly sensing the stiffening of his men. How do they know about this, he thinks. And worse still, the translator, a slave, goes with his answer over the rebuke of a Consul, without that he, Crassus, has a possibility to punish him, as it would be customary, as it would be necessary. The whole familiar world seems to be at an end here. He should never have agreed to a negotiation. Sargon's questions about Aristotle cross his mind. It must not be, all this must not be. He searches for words, he has to answer, he has to respond to the objection, and yet he has to avoid it. If he doesn't, he finally raises the slaves to eye level, under the eyes of his commanders. But should everything fail, he will impose his will on the negotiation, he has made sure of that. »Your doom is sealed«, he retorts sharply, »your supplies have collapsed, there won't be any ships! We have the better weapons. Think about my offer.«

»You can't win any more«, replies the translator, without passing Crassus's words to the Thracian, without turning to him, if only to consult with him. Crassus wants to intervene, but fears speaking into the void and thus making this negotiation fully his defeat.

»Slave-Being is a forced form of life«, the translator continues, »not a form by itself, not of its own accord. By fighting and defeating you, we bring this truth to light. If we surrender, we are already dead today.«

»Only you believe that, and even that I doubt. The truth you speak of will perish with you, that much is certain.«, Then he points his arm at the Thracian. »You there! I offer once more! Surrender and a hundred of your men are free. The rest are left to our mercy.«

With a gesture of despair, the Thracian grips the reins of his horse and Crassus feasts on the emotional outburst. All uncertainty, all confusion in him are flooded by the feeling of superiority and strength.

»We fight«, is then the answer to him. Before he can reply anything, they turn their horses to leave, but trombones are to hear suddenly, Crassus gave them the arranged sign. In an instant, the roman cavalry appears in the back of the Thracian and his companions.

Tense, almost trembling from the aftershock of his recent edification, Crassus waits for the Thracian's next move, eager for his next reaction, as if the previous one had revived parts of his being that greedily announce their thirst.

The cavalry moves closer, but the group around the Thracian remains in a waiting position. Suddenly, the roman cavalry stops abruptly, and made Crassus's limbs schudder. He turns his head and looks at a long line of enemy horsemen behind them. His officers, his legates, he will ask everyone how this could have happened. Yet all questions, all digging and searching, useless at this moment, for he will have to let him go.

*

Crassus follows the Thracian southwest into the rocky land of the Bruttians. Painfully, marked by the strains of the campaign, the legionnaires drag themselves over muddy-clay paths and stony passes. The supply is poor, rain and cold do the rest. Dense wafts of fog lie over the landscape this morning when the vanguard discovers a special find. Crassus, accompanied by his bodyguard, lets himself be led to the designated area. Off the trail, up a gentle hill, among trees and shrubbery, lie several graves, the earth still fresh, the tablets inscribed. On one they read:

> HERE RESTS OUR BELOVED MOTHER
> AND MY BELOVED WIFE.
> IN LOVING MEMORY
> OF YOUR COMFORTING HANDS,
> YOUR DEVOTED AFFECTION FOR YOURS,
> WE BID YOU FAREWELL.

»How many of these graves have you been able to find?«
»About forty to fifty graves«, replied one of the men.
»With stone tablets?«
»Yes. All with tablets and inscriptions. Words of mourning and farewell.«

Crassus takes a few steps. Pushing shrubbery aside, he looks at more tablets. »It's no coincidence«, he finally says to his

men, »that they're buried right here. Look how mystical this little copse is in the landscape.«

He senses his men's discomfort. The Roman-Gods-World leaves plenty of room for superstition. »Have all the tablets removed from the graves«, he says to them nonetheless, »and take down the stones.«

»Consul, we should not disturb the rest of the dead.«

»My dear Scrofa, you are not superstitious, are you? Know that I am not. The dead are dead, but the world is roman and it will remain so. There is no place here for the death cult of slaves.«

His horse is brought up. Annoyed, he rejects the helping hands and gets himself laboriously into the saddle. Then he speaks to Scrofa once more: »Consider above all what these graves still bear witness to after years. There are people and there are slaves! But these graves say otherwise.«

*

Again he fought against him, and though the losses of his army were less, he was not able to defeat him. With forces, with will, with forces that are never constantly available, the insurgents managed to escape the threatening encirclement and to flee to the mountainous hinterland. *About so*, thinks Crassus, they must have fought with the same fierce determination at their outbreak in Capua. *Perhaps, right now, ›he‹ is thinking of that, too.* But this time it shall be of no use to them, for Bruttium measures only forty miles in the middle, from the north to the south shore. And it is there that he, Crassus, will dig a trench and have an oversized wall erected,

to encircle them for good. May they hope to cross from Rhegium to Sicily, - in vain. For he has already warned the Sicilians, as well as the Rhegini, ordered them to refuse landings, remove ships from their ports, reinforce guards. He has thought of everything, all roads closed, all options locked, only a matter of time before the Thracian has to face him.

He rides along a track on which work has already begun. Again, his thoughts twist around the final minutes of the last battle. Confident of victory, he and his officers awaited the end of the war. But the Thracian fought himself, far ahead, and his troops followed him as if they did not know death, executing tactical manoeuvres at a speed that must impress any commander. And Crassus knows that this cannot have escaped the attention of his tribunes.either. Even if they don't say it openly, it is noticeable in the concerns that are expressed, indications of possible dangers regarding their own actions. He then pulls himself together to put an end to these senseless thoughts and concentrates on the wall again. His eyes meticulously search the bulwark or look beyond it, to see if the enemy is making itself felt anywhere, if he is trying to fill in the trench somewhere or tear down the rampart.

*

Another month has passed, a month of waiting for the Thracian, driven by hunger and the desperation of his people, to offer him battle. Just don't risk anything, Crassus thinks. Too easily he could be ambushed in the rocky and valley-strewn country.

Scouts stop in front of his tent, Crassus waves them over. The men look exhausted and sullen. The rain that has been falling for days, whipped up by strong winds, has soaked them completely. Shivering all over, they stand before him. Their faces drawn by the exertions, briefly the report of the Centurion to him: »Nothing happens«, he says with a shrug, »during the day they behave quietly, whether and how many supplies they still have, we do not know. The inhabitants of the land say that they themselves are already starving. At night he has great fires kindled.«

»Have you been able to learn whether many new slaves have joined him?«, asks Crassus.

»There are escapes from the lands. Quite numerous, so it's said.«

With a short nod, he dismisses the legionnaires.

*

The sound of the tarpaulin reminds Cato of his time as a hostage of the insurgents, only the beats are brighter, more thunderous, for the storm is stronger. Again, he tears open the entrance, which servants hurriedly close. Then again, Crassus' voice:: »Perhaps a thousand or two thousand«, he says half to himself, half facing his commander. »There won't be more, this area is not that densely populated.«, His gaze rests on the map. »Well then, leave me alone. Not you yet, Cato. Stay a moment!«, and waits until he is alone with him in the tent.

»You have been with us now since the beginning of the campaign. It's coming to an end. We've constricted the Thracian, basically he's beaten«, he pauses and takes a step toward Cato. »His people are starving, he will give up. Don't you think so too?«

»No.«

»No? Why? Tell me!«, Cato wants to answer, but suddenly - wild shouts, overlapping, croaking voices of exhausted men trying to make themselves understandable, in the storm that has been going on for days. Crassus rushes out, a fierce gust catches him and whips the rain into his face. Protectively, he raises a hand and grasps the tent poles as not to lose his grip. Rain veils pass him by, but he can see the men and hears their shouts. Crassus winces, anything they may say but this. He continues to fight his way through the howling storm, Scrofa close behind him. Some legionnaires have thrown themselves in the mud because of exhaustion. He grabs one by his shoulders, roars at him, as if to tame the storm too: »By all the gods, what has happened!?«

»Consul, he's breaking through«, he replies, panting, »breakthrough! About five miles from here.«

»Have you lost your mind«, he keeps roaring at him, but the storm tears the words away from his mouth. He throws the legionary aside, fights his way back to the tent, reaches for the leashes and roaring out in fury into the storm: »He has to bow! Why doesn't he bow?«

*

The army of insurgents moves east, along the same route they passed through two months ago, passing a copse growing on a gentle hill. It is cold and foggy. This time they advance faster, - the breakthrough was of heavy losses.

Crassus follows with his legions. When they reach the Valley of the Bruttians again, it is littered with crosses from which roman legionnaires are hanging. In a fit of rage and desperation, he drives his troops on a forced march to catch up with the Thracian and forcing him to battle.

Again and again there are small skirmishes and he orders his legions left and right over the hills to heckle him, even it turns out as completely useless. But then it finally seems to succeed, for the baggage train with the women and children, threatens to get stuck in swampy terrain.

He tries to pull together his legions, towards the swampy terrain, yet, spread between the hills, they obstruct each other on their way back, take false passes or get themselves into danger of sinking. After three days, he gives up the futile undertaking.

Chapter 15.

The End

Cato finds the city fathers of Velia in great agitation.

»They have murdered Tiberius«, replies one of the prefects, whom he asks for a brief explanation.

»When?«

»I don't know. The insurgents have moved through Bruttium. It was said you'd tied them up tight, and now this! It was said that you had dug a trench so deep and so wide that it was believed you intend to give the Bruttians a new island, and even with that you couldn't stop the Thracian. Shame on you!«

Cato lets the mockery pass on himself unmoved, it would be pointless to answer. He wants to ask about Tiberius, for he remembers only the name at first, but then the image of a white-haired old senator, with a protruding nose, comes to mind, known for his cruel treatment of his female slaves. *If anyone deserves it*, Cato thinks, but keeps it to himself.

Someone calls for the prefects, as a group of horsemen has just arrived, with the administrator of Tiberius' villa.

Cato follows them into the conference room, which is also used for judicial hearings. It is usually half full, says one of the prefects, addressing Cato as he walks awkwardly beside him: »Common people«, the prefect continues, »officials accompanied by their clients and slaves.« He breaks off abruptly, as he only wanted to cover the few steps into the hall. Cato gazes around. At the back of the hall, slightly shielded, sits a scribe. Numerous papyrus scrolls lie spread out in front of him. To his left, an oversized shelf, in which about a hundred of these note-storing scrolls. His eyes return to the scribe, who has begun to write down the administrator's words.

»His estate is burnt to the ground«, says the administrator.

»What about the slaves?«

»Yes, - about two hundred in all, average age twenty«, the steward replies.

The scribe takes notes on a papyrus scroll, his mouth pointedly formed into an ›O‹, his gaze always scanning the scroll thoughtfully, his hand moves as slowly as if it wanted to learn to write anew.

Cato is still with the administrator's ›yes‹, that short ›yes‹ with which he began his answer. A ›yes‹ that is supposed to create distance, the answer of a person who suspects what's going to happen next. A ›yes‹ like: ›Yes, I'm listening, yes, I'm willing to provide information, that's why I'm here, you see, but I have nothing to do with all this.‹

»Pretty boys and girls, no older than twelve« suddenly comes cheerfully from one of the bystanders, right into the embarrassed silence disturbed only by the scratching of the pen.

»Shut up, you imbecile«, one of the prefects orders him. But the latter goes on, as if the admonition has another meaning, in his mind: »They were trained to suck his stalk, under water.«

»Guards! Get that creature out of here!«

»And now he hangs on the cross?« asks Cato, and all eyes turn to him.

»Yes«, replies the ›imbecile‹. »Now he hangs on the cross and so does his stalk, but in his mouth.« With oblique look and droll laughter, the 'troublesome creature' is carried out by the guards.

One of the prefects, struggling to keep his composure, shouts through the meeting hall to admonish the guards, but in a brittle voice: »This man is of sick mind. Perhaps Zeus hit him with his lightning bolts or perhaps he just ate too many worms that broke down his brain, I don't know. But if I find him here again, it will be your bodies that worms will make their way through!«

Cato watches the prefect's squirming in his chair, after his admonishing words that don't quite want to fit, in this courtroom.

*

Sargon

»Where is Jabulus?«, asks Cato.

»Traveling«, Sargon answers shortly, not yet knowing how to fill Cato in.

»Traveling?«, repeats Cato.

»He sends word to the Cilicians.«

»You're sending word to the Cilicians?«

»Yes.«

Cato stares at his uncle. The concern, the fear Sargon felt upon his return from insurgent captivity. His urging to return to the army as soon as possible to report to Crassus of the Thracian's intention to procure ships in Velia, all present, and now he sends word to the Cilicians. But his unusual posture, his short answer to this question, quickly gives him the certainty that his short ›yes‹ hides more than just the change of mind of some old senator. »You don't have to tell me«, Cato tries to placate. He doesn't believe that placation is necessary, he just wants to add something to his questions in order not to appear silently waiting and thus urgent.

»Come here, my dear. Come, sit down. If they discover Jabulus, torture him, it'll all fall on me. You have nothing to fear, and no one else. You were in the roman army, escorted on your way here - impossible to make contact with the Cilicians.«

»But why?«, Cato asks gently. »What are you planning?«

»Didn't you wish they might make it, over the Alps? And Mirsa? And the aristotelian school, didn't you talk about it, when you said goodbye to Miriam? If they succeed this time, - a blow against this school of thought. And let's hope that Mirsa is still with them and nice and well.«

Sargon leans back with a typical gesture that is supposed to express calm and contentment, but today it doesn't want to succeed. Cato's trying to sort out what he just heard..

Miriam, Mirsa, school of thought ›should they make it this time...‹ remains in his ear. »What, what are you planning?«, he asks patiently, since his uncle seems almost a stranger to him. This old man who usually speaks from a deep, firm spirit, today so brittle, so fragile, says things as if he wants to break with everything, but still leave something good for his own.

»I want the Cilicians to leave their ships to the Thracian, in the port of Brindisi.« Sargon looks into Cato's incredulous startled face. »You don't even ask who is to pay them?«

»No - I...«

»The Cilicians will not follow any request. No, they won't. But if they receive word from Rome, without a seal of course, you see I have not gone entirely mad. A message that ponders on what might possibly await them, when the insurrection is put down and two roman armies, dozing away, await a new task, and what might that be, if not to finally combat the plague of the sea. So if they help the insurgents, leave them ships in Brindisi, and bring them back north, say as far as Ravenna, they'll make it over the Alps this time. The insurrection will gain strength there again, and we will send Pompey to fight him.«

»And Crassus?«

»Crassus' legions will not be sent against the Cilicians; they will be kept here for fear of a new uprising.«

Cato pauses, uncertain whether to ask further. Sargon's words understandable as ever, yet as unreal as his way of speaking is today.

»A strengthening of the insurrection beyond the Alps, was that not what you feared as much as any other senator?«, he asks, ready to take the question back immediately, for he suddenly senses Sargon's tension at the duty to fill him in, without burdening him with it.

»I don't think it will happen anymore«, says Sargon, »but the Cilicians will believe it. When I feared this, - at that time the Thracian had just struck down Gellius and Lentulus, our two consular armies. A wave of enthusiasm would have welcomed him beyond the Alps. And all the discord, all the feuds, all the suspicions that exist between the tribes in the north, he could have united. But today, – the Thracian and all who are with him, have been fighting against our legions for three years. Three years, Cato, that's a long time. Three years of misery, always on Death's side, always on the run. After each battle share the suffering of the prodigal son, the father, the mother.

241

So when they come across the Alps, these people won't incite anyone.

They will be listened to, with curiosity, as one listens to refugees, - nothing more.«

Nothing more, Cato repeats in his mind, as Sargon stops abruptly, but mainly because of the way he uttered the two words, as if this ending pains him.

Sargon looks at his nephew with a smiling face, for nothing should weigh on him. Light-heartedness is what has to be sent out now. It's his work, he hadn't told him anything beforehand and nothing could be more terrible than turning to him, the younger one, for support. »If I'm wrong«, he continues, for he suspects what question moves Cato, »if, then, beyond the Alps the insurrection should grow again, Pompey will actually be sent. And that will be good for all of us. If he and Crassus stay here, each with an army of over 60,000 men, - stupid ideas will jumping up their minds, and not only in them. Whispers from all sides. The sooner one of them has to leave, the better.« Again he stops abruptly, as if he needed a break. Then he turns his gaze back to Cato. »I don't see joy in your face?«

Cato puts on a brief embarrassed smile, as if to follow his wish comfortably, but immediately regrets it, knowing that Sargon will always refuse comfort. He suddenly senses how much he must have struggled with himself. Sees the courage it takes to rise above all the uncertainty. He sits down next to him. »A hit against the aristotelian school«, he says then, reaching for his hand.

»Yes, yes, it will be so.«

*

242

Horsemen appear on the Via Appia to Rome, whipping their horses, couriers from Crassus' army. Quickly the guards open the Porta Capena, the horsemen rush through, without greeting, without the usual formalities, because they bring news that could hardly be more terrible.

Message for the Aerarii Militaris,

Cilicians might supply ships,

In the port of Brindisi,

Lucullus possibly too late,

Urgently advise:

　　Pompejus back north

　　surrounding area of Ravenna.

M. L. Crassus

The Aerarii Militaris are hastily convened by the Senate, the nobility excluded. Urgency, horror and consternation leave no space for lengthy pros and cons. It is quickly agreed that Pompey should not advance any further, and that he needs to send back north, at least half of his troops.

*

Escape

Crassus divides his army again and has Scrofa pursue the Thracian with the main force. He himself wants to call in new troops from the cities of the northern Bruttium. *There is still time, two weeks, perhaps three*, he thinks. *May the Thracian*

drive his people, forced march, day and night. With his train of women and children, the route will demand this time. He hopes to challenge him once more, and then, with a triple superiority, to overthrow him definitively. His victory, it needs to be, has to be, must be, not that of Pompey or Lucullus. Threateningly, he shows the prefects what penalties they will face. The war will be over one way or another, but they will question Bruttium's allegiance if they don't hand over troops to him.

After assembling two legions from the new troops, he follows the Quaestor who, according to his legates, has now reached the flat land south of Genusia.

When the view of the valley opens, they see their own men in wild escape running towards them. Crassus, realizing the situation, orders battle formation, has the trombones sounding, to signal safety for the fleeing men, and summons Scrofa immediately, who reports with halting words, almost tearfully:

»We followed him, as you said, always captured smaller groups and always kept at our distance. I didn't think he'd fight us again, but suddenly we had him in front of us, in full battle formation. They fell upon us with such fury I could not hold our men back. Forgive me, Consul.«

Crassus, beside himself with rage, orders the legions to form in a semicircle and threatens to subject them to another decimation, if they should flee out of cowardice again.

*

The Thracian moves on with his troops as soon as the terrain allows, no longer mindful of hiding, only further, further to the port of Brundisium.

*

remember

»Sertorius, a courier has just arrived with news from Crassus.«

»Once again! Is the whole army made up of couriers?« With a dismissive hand gesture he then adds: »Let him in.«

The courier enters the room, bows and hands over the message. Sertorius, half-over-flying the papyrus and muttering with his lips the seemingly important places before him, passes the letter on to his four brothers in office. Patiently he waits until the last one has read the letter.

»Well«, says Sertorius, »I think we can say that this is probably the end.«

»What if he moves north again?«

»He won't do that. We made the right decision a week ago. Pompey is only a day south of Rome and I'm sure the Thracian knows this. And if I read correctly, the riffraff is moving across the Apennines in forced marches to reach the port of Brindisi, the last straw left to them. If they keep up this pace, which I doubt after the famine days, they could be there in a week. But even if they manage the impossible again this time - Lucullus will disembark there in the next few days, Crassus is following them. When the pack gets there and realizes there aren't any ships, they are caught between two armies. And even this Spartacus will be finished then.«

All are silent.

»Yes, it will be the end for him«, Sargon breaks the silence first. »Let's hope, our efforts to destroy him won't make him more remembered, than us.«

Out of the corner of his eye, he watches the rolling of eyes, the heads turning back and forth, but he shows no sign of satisfaction.

»Yes, it will be the end for him«, Sargon breaks the silence first. »Let's hope, that our efforts to destroy him, won't make him more remembered, than us.« Out of the corner of his eye, he watches the eye rolling, the turning of their heads back and forth, regardless he doesn't show any sign of satisfaction.

He rises, without any theatrics. »For an old man, it is time to go. Since all the slaves who are after our lives will soon be recaptured, I think we can sleep more soundly again.«

»Sargon«, Sertorius calls, rising and walking slowly towards him to continue in a bitter voice: »I shall never understand why a man born on the banks of the Tiber has sympathy for this vermin.«

Sargon, already past the threshold of the exit, turns once more. »It doesn't matter. There is much you don't understand.«

*

Crassus follows the Thracian without haste, knowing that he cannot escape him.

After four days, scouts return and report that the Cilicians had tried to land at Brindisi, but Lucullus had already disembarked. The insurgents stopped short of Brindisi. For a day and a night they did not move. At first the scouts believed that now, completely demoralised, they had given up and were awaiting death. But despite their forced march and the bad weather, they have risen again and are on the march towards this camp.«

*

»Crassus, the battle has lasted almost ten hours, the men are finished.«

»I know that. Regardless I want every surviving slave captured, the more the better. About five legions lie dead on the battlefield...«, he stops abruptly, the entrance opens and Cato enters the tent. »Therefore«, he continues, »everyone who can move shall help to find the wounded and.«

»Consul«, Cato interrupts, almost in a whisper, and their eyes meet, »we're still fighting.«

Crassus raises his head, slowly, as if all the burden, all the despair of this war were wrapped around his neck. »What' you say?«, he asks with a dry throat. »Are you still with you?«

»There are about a thousand«, Cato says in reply. »He's in it, too.«

»HE? - Who is HE? - Has HE no name?« Crassus walks slowly towards Cato. »Where? Where is he?«

Cato rides ahead, Crassus closely behind him. The battle lasted ten hours, four times during that time he brought in fresh forces. Most legionnaires can last five hours... Crassus forces his mind on the path before them, on Cato's horse, on everything that moves, but he can't stop this spirit in him...only a few manage six... Pain in the wrists... Fingers weakened, shield and sword are hard to hold, but those there are still fighting.

The insurrection passes him by, from the beginning of his meeting with Sargon. And there is Aristotle again, there is his meeting with Annaeus, all the conversations, all the thoughts seem to rear up inside him...and it is better for them, better for

them.... in this kind of servitude...well taken care of, then, for their own well-being. But those there are still fighting.

Those there...to whom life becomes an unbearable burden, fight like these...life a burden, in the servitude which is meant to be the best for them. Crassus reins in his horse to have it walk sideways Cato's.

Dusk is already falling as they look down on the fighters from the crest of a hill, shifting winds carry the sounds very clearly: the bright thudding sound of swords, the cracking sound of bones bursting, and the moaning and groaning of the dying.

»You admire him, don't you, Cato?« Sober, without any particular emphasis on a word, Crassus asks him the question, also keeping his gaze straight ahead.

»He deserved to be born a roman«, Cato replies.

»I'm not asking what he deserves, I'm asking if you admire him«, he repeats, deliberately emphatic, **for** he suspects that the question must agitate him. **For** he, Crassus, asks him this question, he insinuates the possibility of admiration for a runaway slave, an enemy of Rome. **For**, admiration for Hannibal, even for him, openly expressed, was considered treason.

Crassus turns his face to see in his, and recognizes the fright in Cato's countenance, regardless his trial to hide it, but he holds his gaze and answers: »Before the battle began, he spoke to his men. He said that today was the decisive battle. In front of them would be Crassus, in the back Lucullus. They must either win and destroy Crassus' legiones or perish together. Then they brought up his horse, a black Numidian steed that had been his since the beginning of the insurrection, and he stabbed it with his sword. He held it by the reins

and stabbed it, three times in the chest. Then he called out to them that he doesn't need a horse today. If he were to win,

he would take one of the enemies. In the event of a downfall, he would not need one today or ever again. Then they stormed on us. So if you ask me, Consul, the answer is yes. Yes, I admire him!«

Crassus gives no answer. Silently, sitting on his horse, he remains beside him. After a while he asks him another question:

»How do you know what he said?«

»One of our men, who fought in the front line, told me. I don't know how he knows, no one speaks that language. But it's already being told everywhere.«

Although the story of the Spartacus insurrection, on which the novel is based, is historically proven, this version is also based on fictional elements.

The following quotations were used in the novel:

The report of the Greek historian and geographer Agatharchides. from: „*Weber, Slavery in Antiquity*" p. 186f.

Aristotle, quoted from: Lautemann/Schlenke, „*Geschichte in Quellen*" p. 311.

Alkidamas, quoted from: Weber, „*Sklaverei im Altertum*", p. 331.

Hippias of Elis, quoted from: Kanz, „*Vorsokratische Denker*", p. 221.